SLAVE KING
Rebels Against Empire

A Novel By **BASEM L. RA'AD**

Daraja Press

Published by
Daraja Press
https://darajapress.com

© 2023 Basem L. Ra'ad

ISBN: 978-1-990263-52-1

Library and Archives Canada Cataloguing in Publication

Title: Slave king: rebels against empire: a novel / Basem L. Ra'ad.
Names: Ra'ad, Basem L., author.
Identifiers: Canadiana 2022040657X | ISBN 9781990263521 (softcover)
Classification: LCC PS8635.A223 S53 2022 | DDC C813/.6—dc23

SLAVE KING
Rebels Against Empire

Prologue

Enna
c. 140 BCE

Every day before dawn, before anyone stirs, he is awakened by premonitions. He goes out into the half-darkness, circles the citadel, and walks down the hill toward the escarpment past the sad dark-green cypresses lining the path. He then stands at the head of a rock that juts out into the escarpment like a god extending a hand to some source.

Every day he looks toward the distant east from whence he came, wondering what the future might hold, and waiting in gratitude for the daily return of the sun. At night, he has dreams of men and women gathered in multitudes, melding into a single will. The men are holding him high on their shoulders, cheering as they carry him along. Beyond them, a group of children are decked in spring-flowers, and a girl holds a magical green branch presaging a bountiful future of plenty. 'Aṭirat appears in her glory to place a wreath on his head and release a white dove into the horizon. 'Aṭirat, Ašera and 'Aštart, Inanna and Iset, who gave birth to 'Anat and Tanīt, Aphrodite and Venus, who later became Atargatis and Dea Syria, each and all facets of the Great Mother. 'Aṭirat, she is here to tell him his purpose, listen to his prayers and be with him in the events that wait to happen.

He has witnessed this same dawn day after day for years. Without fail he looks to the south, imagining that he can see beyond the sea to Qart Ḥadašt, which Roma called Carthago, and remembers its days of prosperity. But Qart Ḥadašt is no more, except in the memory of those who loved it and live on as slaves, some even on this island. As the sun begins to rise, he turns toward the east, toward home.

There was a day as clear as this when he was about six, more than twenty years before. His mother, Maryam, a shadow smile on her face, held his right hand, and with her deep black eyes looked tenderly into his hazel eyes. She stroked his densely coiled hair, not yet as dark as now, and told him how he was birthed a month after his father Aqbar's death in the wars. Filled with more grief than hope, she laboured and he entered the world auspiciously at dawn.

She dedicated him to the Great Goddess as the only child who would regale her and keep her company in old age. That is why she gave him the name Younis, one who entertains, keeps company and consoles the spirit. It is the name of the man in legend who is swallowed and vomited out whole by a sea creature. Ten years after his forced removal from Afamia, the columns he gaped at in wonder as he walked its thoroughfare were now shrouded in dark memory. He last glimpsed their rhythmic spiral flutes through the bars of a carriage as it sped away in fog and rain toward the slave ships on the coast.

Chapter 1

Afamia
c. 150 BCE

Thirteen boys, aged fifteen to seventeen, sat in a semi-circle, listening to their teacher, Mani. Mani came from Antiokia and had spent some years in Athênai, where he was a student at its academy, taught there for a short time, and visited Thêbai. The schoolroom was large and airy, with a high ceiling studded with round wooden beams. Shafts of mid-morning light filtered through the two windows to the south. From the opposite windows came distant sounds of children playing. As usual, Mani was installed on a cushion almost in the corner in front of a wall mosaic where a nymph played the lyre as birds perched on a tree. The boys sat around him cross-legged on reed mats, insufficient protection against the cold of early spring seeping through the limestone floor.

They took turns reading aloud scenes of the play *Phoinissai* by Euripides from manuscripts they had copied the previous week. The day before, they had recited poems from Qart Ḥadašt, whose writings they were keen to explore. Mani stopped reading after the chorus of Phoínikē women appeared and conflict between the two sons of Oidipous emerged.

He asked in Aramaic: "In what ways is the chorus of women dramatically important? Some have said that despite the title, the chorus has no real role or involvement in the play."

"Doesn't the chorus wish that no harm should come to the city and its people, and so provide a kind of antidote to this tragic prospect?" remarked Asur, the smallest but most talkative among the youth. "After all, the chorus says any harm would affect them too. That's dramatic involvement."

"True," Mani said. "The chorus, while neutral to the action, embodies values of equality and justice, tries to prevent conflict, and establishes the setting by making the connection between Thê-bai and its predecessors on our coast. About the rising conflict, the chorus says that 'fairness and equality have no existence in this world beyond name.' If the world is filled with injustice, violence and chaos ensue."

"The chorus also declares: 'Our blood is one'. Is that not significant?" asked Zarak, nicknamed Zuzu, who stood out for his very blonde hair.

"Yes, the same blood. It was still early enough for the Hellenes to recognise their debt and true relationship to people from a region of Cana'an they called Phoínikē, the land of purple dye and palms. The Hellenes owe a lot to them—to us, that is."

For Mani, the play's setting in Thêbai provided an opportunity to tell his students about the city's founder, called Kadmos by the Hellenes. He was an ancestor of Oidipous, the one fated to commit a most primal and horrible sin. Mani wanted to explain how Kadmos' real name, without the Greek ending, would have been something like *q-d-m*, probably meaning 'the one arriving' in Cana'anite. Kadmos was said to have carried the alphabet for the Hellenes to write their language, and several myths had emerged about him. Was his sister Europa abducted by Zeus, the Ba'al of the Hellenes, who had transformed himself into a bull to approach her? And was her name, Europa, itself a symbolic variation of Ghourba, meaning 'evening' or 'setting sun' in Cana'anite? His daughter Semelē was said to have conceived the god Dionysos, the Greek version of 'Adōn or Tammūz, from the seed of Zeus. Were these ways for Hellenes to attach our mythology to their reality, joining gods and mortals into their own vision of unity?

"There is so much on these matters that is hidden, and much of what people say today may have been altered with the passage of time," Mani began. "The history may never be completely uncovered, yet there are . . . "

His words were interrupted as all turned toward the sound of the heavy wooden door being slung open and the stomping of soldiers walking toward them. Mani stood up hurriedly, a silent panic on his face. The entire class was struck dumb. Mani suspected that these men had come to take away some of his young charges to meet the demands of a humiliating treaty Roma had imposed after their king's defeat three decades ago. It required a sizeable tribute, hostages and slaves. Later on, the senate in Roma incited pretenders to the crown to fight amongst themselves in order to wreak havoc in the kingdom, a kingdom shrunken in all directions from its large extent after Alexandros. Mani stood and stared, impotent before the soldiers, and unable to do anything to protect his beloved students.

Five helmeted soldiers, clad in blue and red and carrying sarissas, were escorted by a man with a pointed beard and quick shifting eyes. He did not wear military dress but a tight brown kaftan of thick cotton with a leather girdle and a long odd tawny cloak.

The pointy-bearded man barked, "Stand up!" He waited for all to stand.

"I am Makedo, servant of His Majesty King Alexandros Theopator Balas. He has entrusted me with the task of selecting from amongst you those who will serve the kingdom."

Makedo inched closer, his eyes searching. He pointed deliberately at four boys, who were then each seized by the soldiers. He peered now at Younis, who was near Mani. Makedo moved closer— so close that his hair nearly grazed Younis' shoulder. Perhaps it was the young man's unusual appearance that attracted Makedo's attention: dark coiled bush of hair, sharp dark hazel eyes, two slight bony nubs on the forehead, a prominent nose and large nostrils. Younis had a body of average build, but he was broad-shouldered. Muscular strength already showed in his hairy legs and arms.

"What is your name, boy?"

"My name is Younis," he replied defiantly, standing upright with his feet slightly parted, though his heart was thumping. His instincts told him that something was amiss, that this man was not up to any good. He had just turned seventeen. The pointed beard nodded to a soldier, who quickly approached and grabbed Younis by the arm. None of the boys put up any struggle, seemingly paralyzed by shock at what was unfolding around them. Mani attempted to intercede, careful not to anger the man or the soldiers.

"We should inform the families before you take these boys. They must know," he said somewhat lamely.

Makedo was dismissive. "You can inform them yourself later on." He handed Mani a scroll, "For now, write down these boys' names and affix your seal. We need everything to be in order." Another command Mani was powerless to refuse.

The boys were led away into the yard, marching in the drizzle toward a four-horse carriage. Dark clouds threatened heavier rain. Their sandals scraped heavily on the cobble stones as they were shoved into a cage-like covered wagon. Inside, ten boys were already seated on the two benches and the floor. Before a word could be uttered, the horses were whipped and the carriage drove out of sight.

Racing up and down hills along rocky roads, the carriage sped away in the rain to Laodikea, intent on making up enough time to arrive before sunset. Despite the noise, silence reigned among the captives. What could anyone say or do in such an unexpected situation? Younis turned to ask one of the boys where they were going and what had happened to them, shouting to be heard above the roar of wheels and hooves. The boy told him they were all classmates taken from their school. They were forbidden from speaking to anyone or even seeing their families before they were hauled away.

A few hours on, a rancid stink pervaded the carriage. With no windows or even spaces between the bars large enough to put their heads out, two boys had vomited on the floor. Some others, as young as twelve or thirteen, sobbed openly. Most sat silently, tears coursing down their cheeks. Younis was not crying. He thought only of his mother. Mani would have told her and the other families by now. All the families would surely be mourning too, the whole village resentful and in distress. He felt sick thinking about what could happen to her, living in such all-consuming sorrow. He imagined her weeping to the skies, calling upon the goddesses, and spending long days and nights in worry and despair. Without him, there was no one left to ease her life's pain, nowhere to seek refuge, and only endless grief manifested in floods of tears and desolate wails. Old age would arrive quickly, and treat her cruelly.

As night approached, they could smell the sea. The carriage stopped near tens of others jostling for space on the crowded port. They strained to get a better view of the ships through the carriage boards. Fresh air finally blew in as the door of the cage flung open. The guards, sticks and daggers in hand, separated the boys and prepared them to be taken to sea. Younis could smell the smoke of meat being grilled and hear the hiss of steam from pots, but no food was offered to them as they waited. He was prodded to join a group already on the dock, a gaggle of captive adults and children. They spoke agitatedly above the noise, sometimes in Aramaic, sometimes in Greek. Younis could sense their confusion and fear. A harsh oppression reigned that the mild sea breeze could not ease. As they were led onto a ship, he overheard the guards speaking of Delos as their destination. Younis had heard rumours about Delos and its auctions. With dread, he realised that their captivity would either be long or permanent. Those forced into that doom had seldom been heard from again, vanishing into an absence more silent than death.

Chapter 2

Passers-by used to go to his mother to inquire as to what he was doing, seeing the boy perched high atop a rock scratching something on his lap. He used a sharpened piece of charcoal to scribble on small fragments of papyrus, which he sometimes later rewrote in a permanent ink made from soot or ochre mixed with gum arabic and vegetable oils. There he stayed, writing even after dusk, so absorbed that he did not notice their hurried passing or the approaching darkness.

"What are you writing, my Younis?" Maryam asked when he returned. "People become curious when they see you on the hill. Perhaps you write those predictions you keep making about the weather and what is to happen. Be careful, or people will look at you as if you have come from another world," she added with a slight smile.

He reassured her. "No, mother, don't worry. Predictions and visions are not to be written down. I only write lines of poetry and thoughts I want to commit to memory."

Maryam replied with these words: "I don't worry about you, son. I know you will never be afraid to be true to your calling."

Now, everything had changed. Life itself had ceased, and its promises, hopes and ambitions extinguished so quickly and so inexplicably. It seemed no longer possible to recover those days of poetry and trance, when passions came and inspiration arose without apparent will. This memory was part of his salvation, though he did not tell his mother then that he had shadowy forebodings of an impending separation.

After stops in Kypros and Delos to load more slaves and supplies, the ship continued to its final destination, the port of Missina. It was a hard journey. The ship struggled against turbulent seas and strong spring winds that stretched the journey to more than ten days. More than a hundred women, men and children were packed into the hold, sickened by unfamiliar darkness and angry waves. In addition to its human cargo, the ship was carrying something even more valuable: hundreds of amphorae of Hellas wine, large bags of grain, and what seemed to be huge bolts of fabrics from the East.

Captives were fed twice a day: dry bread in the morning and a stale porridge of barley with remnants of horse meat in the late afternoon. They had two places to relieve themselves, one side for women and another for men, two holes in the corner of the hold separated by canvas sheets. They were ordered to pass water into two buckets and, after defecating into the hole, wipe themselves with a sponge fixed on a stick before rinsing it in a bucket of sea water. Two slaves were assigned to clean around the holes and dump the buckets into the sea twice a day. With all this discharge and frequent vomiting, a putrid stink developed in the hold, and there was almost no way to escape the stench. On evenings, weather permitting, they were taken out in small groups to the deck for brief moments of fresh sea air, intended only to prevent more sickness.

As the ship sailed into the port of Missina, now called Messana, the human cargo was taken up to the deck. Surveying the scene, Younis noticed the harbour's unique sickle shape, which signaled its importance as a strategic location and a point of entry into Sicilia. After disembarking, they were walked through the streets, tied loosely together. Younis was struck by how much of the talk he heard from passers-by was in Greek more than any other language. Their temporary destination was an underground holding area in a large building, which they entered through a prison-like barred gate. It was completely bare except for dirty mats and blankets spread out on the cold stone floor. There were five large caged rooms on one side of the hold, and four huge troughs in the middle.

In the next two days, the slaves were prepared for auction. They were groomed and coached on how to stand, behave, and respond to commands and questions. Men, women and children were bathed in the troughs, several at a time. Water was not changed in the troughs, only topped up with warm water when needed. The traders were aware that expending some additional effort to prepare their human cargo would result in more profit, and were meticulous in examining all of them one by one to determine their value. Mouths were opened, teeth counted, eyes and ears prodded, genitals examined for cleanliness and appearance. The captives were then oiled, perfumed, and given clean linen tunics. When necessary, the traders used a paste of gall and liver or other concoctions to improve looks or to cover imperfections. They argued among themselves over merits and defects. A prime young female with ample breasts and a fine figure was estimated to be worth at least twenty thousand sestertii, probably more to start, whereas an older man with no particular skills to offer except hard labour might not fetch more than three or four thousand, if that. Wooden plaques were hung around their necks describing their place of origin, age, and any special skills or abilities. Plaques for young women were explicit in promoting pleasures for the prospective owner. A woman next to Younis wore a plaque that read: "Kilikian maid not yet 20 years. Perfect skin, ample bosom, beautiful eyes, warm body, useful in kitchen and bed." An older woman was promoted as an excellent cook, another as skillful in child-rearing, or a ready nursemaid.

Younis was assessed to be of good value for a young man, his *natio* vaunted a positive quality, considered cultured and fairly tame. It was an added bonus that he spoke and wrote Greek and had attended school for a number of years, as a potential tutor tended to fetch a high price at auction. His plaque was crafted to attract those interested in finding an attendant for children or even for a master: "Healthy Syrian from the famous city of Apamea. Agile body. Only seventeen years old with more than ten years of schooling. Trained in philosophy, science, and literature. Speaks and writes Aramaic and Greek, reads Latin. Ideal as tutor or companion."

It was a cool spring day when the slaves were taken out for display. Several of them shivered as they walked against a strong breeze. Assembled behind two stands, they were called up to the block two or three at a time. When a name was shouted out by the auctioneer, the slave would be escorted to the centre of the stand, and their tunic pulled off to display their nakedness. Interested buyers approached to inspect every part, including skin, teeth, ears and other cavities. The first two women brought out instinctively moved their hands to cover their lower parts when their tunics were pulled off. They were immediately chided by a man carrying a whip and ordered to leave their arms at their sides. Younis and other men were lucky to avoid this added humiliation, as they were allowed to keep their loincloths.

Sales were brisk, and most captives fetched good prices. Younis was no exception. A middle-aged man approached, inspected his body, touched his arms and muscles of his thighs, pushed down his jaw to look at his teeth, and then spoke in Greek. "What subjects did you study in school? Do you speak Latin?" To the latter, Younis replied that he did read Latin and understood some of it when spoken, enough to improve in a short time. This man won the bidding over two others, purchasing Younis for a price of twelve thousand sestertii.

He tried to be friendly as he escorted Younis to a carriage. "My name is Marius Tullius. I work for the estates owned by our lord Pedanius Antigenes, who lives in the city of Enna. You will be staying at his estate in Messana until we make further arrangements. Your master will decide where you will go and what you will do. I will send a message right away to tell him you are here." Antigenes did not visit this estate frequently, he added. He only came on extremely urgent matters or as a rest stop when traveling to Roma. This estate was one of two he owned, a farm mostly for growing grain and raising cattle for export from the port to the peninsula. Tullius told Younis that he would send a message to tell his master and wait for instructions before transporting him to Enna, probably in ten days or sooner.

Since it became clear that he would not be given any task, on the second day Younis asked Tullius if he could explore the estate. On his first long walk in the fields, he reached a wooded hill and climbed to its top to discover a cave and a rock platform in front with a view of the surrounding fields. He would make it a habit to take water and fruit and go sit at the cave's entrance. As he surveyed the landscape, he was reminded of his homeland. Yesterday he had been reassured of care and love by mother and friends, and at school disputing the mysteries of the past and how to achieve goodness in the present. It was a similar land in its grittiness, but how different the feeling. Today it mirrored his unknown fate, its blankness threatening to consume hope and bring on the lethargy of loss. He asked himself how he could avoid being lulled into accepting such a humiliating condition as one with no alternative. He knew for sure that he could never succumb to despair, cowardice or confusion. He could never allow himself merely to survive and obey mindlessly, his soul kept telling him. But he did not know yet when the meaning lost would be regained, or how his displaced spirit could recover its purpose.

Chapter 3

The gate of Antigenes' mansion was still open when they arrived in late afternoon of the fourth day. As the carriage drove into the spacious courtyard, Younis noticed that the mansion, walled throughout, comprised two buildings. There was a low one on the left, which he later found out contained the kitchens and slave quarters. To the right stood the two-storey residence of the Antigenes family and the *triclinium*, a spacious hall for feasting. Beyond the *triclinium*, a large patio led to the gardens through several meandering walkways paved in flat stones, some with natural striations and designs that one might, upon close examination, easily imagine as outlines of some earthly form, animal, human or inanimate. The gardens contained a variety of fruit-bearing and ornamental trees, beds of flowers and herbs, and two fountains, one of them with a pond. It spread over a large expanse, making up almost half of the entire mansion, and ended at a massive wall at the edge of a precipice on the city's east side.

Several slaves came out to the courtyard to catch a glimpse of the new arrival. Among them was a middle-aged woman who stepped forward to welcome Younis, and introduced herself as Camilla. She took him to the kitchens, offered him a light repast and water, then handed him a mat and cover sheet and showed him a place where he could sleep that night. The next day, at about noon, he was escorted to the library to see the master.

In a room filled with manuscripts organised in compartments on the walls and in earthenware containers, a man was sitting on a cathedra, fully intent on projecting the image of a high-ranking man of means, though it was uncertain whether this display was tempered by humility or simple self-awareness. He had a large head and high brow, straight greying hair receding at the temples, a clean-shaven face, deep-set eyes, and a prominent nose above a small mouth. At first, for an unexplained moment, it seemed that Antigenes was feeling unsure in front of the young slave purchased as a possible tutor. Perhaps it was the young man's countenance and demeanour, his bushy coils and distinctive physical features, or his deliberate posture that gave him pause. He greeted Younis and motioned for him to sit on a stool close by. He looked at him intently, with the shade of a smile. His first questions surprised Younis. He inquired, in apparent concern, about his experiences since leaving his homeland. What did Antigenes imagine Younis must feel about this reversal of fortune? What could he say, it crossed the mind of the young tutor to be, in answer to a man who was trying to be benevolent in this situation? Hesitantly, Younis told Antigenes the bare facts of where he came from, how he was captured and what followed.

"Were you treated well in Messana?" Younis wondered what Antigenes might consider to be good treatment, though he knew enough to give him what he expected to hear, which was not too far from the truth.

"Yes, Tullius was kind and the people were friendly."

"What about your family? Tell me."

"I have some relatives in other towns, and my mother," Younis choked, "I left without her knowing I had been taken. She must be suffering and desolate not knowing where I am."

Antigenes was silent for a moment.

"You must think of her all the time. What about your father?"

"My father was killed in the wars before I was born. I am my mother's only child."

Antigenes seemed moved by this, but made no comment. Instead, he asked practical questions about the education Younis received, obviously to determine if it was sufficient to qualify him as a tutor of his children. Did he not see the irony of putting a would-be tutor through the paces? Someone who might be good enough to teach his children, yet was unworthy of liberty, to be forcibly deprived of family, schooling, friends, community, so that he and his family could benefit? Younis told him that his schooling covered many subjects in the arts and sciences, in both Aramaic and Greek. He mentioned that his abilities in Latin were mostly limited to reading, though his fluency would improve in time. He named a few works of literature and philosophy that he had read, and referred to the great mathematicians from Hellas as well as those from Aígyptos, Sumeria and Syria, where the sciences started, using the names for these regions familiar to Antigenes. Antigenes seemed to be impressed, especially since Younis delivered the information in fluent Greek, of which Antigenes himself had perfect mastery. He explained that Younis' main task would be to teach his two children the rigours of learning and to develop their basic understanding and skills of numbers, arithmetic, reading and writing. He wanted them to become familiar with Hellenic culture, as he recognised the advantage of learning its arts and numbering system, as well as that of other regions, which were different from the standard in Roma. Antigenes appeared to be genuine in his appreciation of the knowledge advances in other cultures.

"Junia is almost eleven years old already and Julian is ten. They had a tutor for more than four years, but he is no longer with us. You will continue with some basic skills for three or four hours a day, as much as you find possible to do with them, and add some readings in literature as you see fit, which will be enough for now. They speak mostly in Greek at home and with friends. Another person has been assigned to continue their lessons in Latin. You will be responsible for the rest. As they get older, we can decide what other subjects to teach them."

"I will try to give them what knowledge I have."

"That will be good. Do you have any questions?"

Younis hesitated, as he turned toward the walls.

"I see all these writings, even more than we had at school. May I be permitted to examine some manuscripts when possible?"

"I have no problem with that," he answered, though he looked a bit taken aback. "It may be helpful in your task. You can come anytime I am not here and on other days when I travel. If you want you can bring the children for some lessons here. I will show you where I leave the key," he added to indicate the meeting was over, "I am sure you will benefit the children and do well as their tutor. Ask Camilla to come and see me."

Younis found out that Antigenes told Camilla to give him his own cella to sleep in. It seemed that Antigenes wanted to reassure him of good treatment, which brought some relief for the first time since his capture. Perhaps he was telling Younis not to blame him personally too much for his captive condition, though as a thoughtful man he must have realised that he was nevertheless part of the system that perpetrated such injustice. At each step, Younis was already trying to understand what it would take to survive and develop his own skills. Perhaps to prosper as well, where in this self-contradictory world he was compelled to play a useful role for the family that had grown prosperous from the labour of slaves— slaves who took away all the drudgery and hard cares of daily life.

He decided to delay the lessons for two days to allow time for preparations, but still went later that day to meet the two children. Though only one year older, Junia struck him as much taller than Julian—a fact exaggerated by her ankle-long tightly belted tunic, which contrasted with Julian's short tunic and his slender legs. Her blonde hair was tied into a loose bun, her face at first sight appeared quite plain, wide nose with large nostrils, below it thin lips almost pursed and a round still undefined chin. She was sprightly and visibly more cheerful than Julian, who had diminutive features and dark brown hair arranged in cornrows. He looked somewhat emaciated and obviously needed more attention to bring him along, something Younis was already determined to attempt. It must have been that many hopes were placed on Julian's shoulders as the male child, but Junia must have already been aware of the uniqueness of her situation. Antigenes was not following the tradition of indifference to a girl's learning, and her cheerfulness may have intuitively acknowledged her privilege relative to other girls.

Younis thought it best to befriend them first and to have them enjoy learning and be eager for it, since it seemed they had previously studied under strict discipline. He took them out to the garden to explore and become more aware of the living world around them, and to talk with them about plants, trees and rocks. He engaged them in trying out geometrical shapes, using strings and common objects, so as to discover basic earthly patterns and principles. To train them further in arithmetical calculation, he devised several problem-solving games and puzzles, though he was very sparing in assigning work with the abacus to which they were accustomed.

It was more difficult to have fun with Greek grammar and writing, to discover the mystery of the language and its uses, and all it held within it. Younis had them read aloud and write on a number of topics, but as they did that, he also found ways to make the shapes of signs in the alphabet memorable. He demonstrated that the characters were more than mere shapes. In fact, if traced to its origins, the alphabet lent itself to a somewhat theatrical demonstration of how the signs derived from common aspects of nature, from parts of the animal or human body, the head, eye, palm of the hand, or waves of the sea, each letter first inspired by the word for an object that starts with that sound. He would stand and act out how the first letter, the *alif,* which comes from *alīf* or domesticated animal, gradually changed from its shape as the head of a godly sacred bull, what better beginning could there be, to become the A that starts the alphabet. The word we use today, "alpha-bet," he told them, combined this *alif* with *beit* or house, which lent its primary shape to the original B. With his palm held high, he would space out and move his fingers to show them how the K grew from its shape as the palm of a hand or *kf* to end up with its simplified three sticks. He traced sea waves in the garden sand to illustrate how the squiggle that stood for the sound M comes from the word for water. Other writing systems, he explained, had been developed elsewhere, such as the sacred writing of Aígyptos, the land its people called Kemet or Miṣru, but they were not as simple and involved hundreds of pictures and signs that were difficult except for scribes and priests. This Cana'anite invention used the idea of pictures but simplified the system by using only 28 signs to represent basic sounds, of which the Greeks used the 24 that their language required. Younis showed Junia and Julian, using a large sheet or sometimes on a patch of sand in the garden, how a few signs were changed in use from their original sounds. The 'ayn, first represented by the shape of an eye, and the strong ḥ, shaped like a ladder, which were not sounds in Greek or Latin, became the vowel O and the letter H. Now, every time Julian and Junia traced a letter they had a story about it and attempted to give each one their own artistic flair.

Since they were writing in both Greek and Latin, Junia asked about the number of letters.

"We have 26 letters in Latin. Why is there a difference between Greek and Latin?"

"The differences are not that many, but they do tell us something. Notice that Greek R looks like P, which goes back to the original shape of a head, ras, as you can see. Differences are there because Latin was taken from another related source. Of course, there's also the cursive script that developed recently."

"Our Latin teacher tried to have us write in cursive. I hate that so much. It's hard to understand the scribbles of people. Some of it looks like the marks hens make in the dirt," Julian remarked.

To explain Younis had to delve into some history. A few hundred years ago the Peninsula was largely made up of Etrusci city states belonging to people who called themselves Rasna. Even Roma itself was founded and ruled at first by Etrusci kings. It was a culture advanced in the arts and letters. The Etrusci, he explained, probably came from other coasts of this Great Sea to the east and established city states on the Peninsula. In time, the Etrusci kings were removed from Roma and instead its powerful inhabitants formed a senate, declaring the city a republic. This new polity over-powered the neighbouring region of Latium, and occupied the other Etrusci city states. As Roma expanded, it also adopted use-ful aspects of Etrusci culture, including the alphabet, the skills of building and some gods, even the national story of a founder who came as a refugee from Troia. The Etrusci letters were written from right to left, a convention probably inspired by the Cana'anites, but when adopted as Latin the direction of writing was reversed.

"I didn't know that. So we took our writing system from the people we destroyed," observed Julia, surprising Younis with the bald manner in which she stated a conclusion that he was trying to suggest tactfully.

"That's what often happens when people are too proud to ad-mit what they have borrowed from others, especially from those they demonise because it becomes more beneficial to see them as enemies. It's sometimes difficult for humans to accept that they depend on each other for knowledge," Younis said, leaving them to ponder.

Before reading longer works of literature and history in their entirety, Younis introduced Junia and Julian to the basics of the art of story-telling. What better start could there be than the symbolic fables of Aisopos. It was not only because they were easy to read but more for lessons they taught using animal characters and plants as covers to expose human frailties and biases in the social order. Aisopos was rumoured to have been a dark-skinned slave, ugly in features, born more than three hundred years before. Some said he came from Aethiopia, while others placed his origins in Lydia or even farther east. Younis told Junia and Julian what could be guessed about his life, from slave to free man, at least what little of it that was likely to be true. His animal fables sometimes reflected on the relationship between slaves and masters. The words of the tales, though, and even the tales themselves may have been modified and added to by later writers. Other tales continued traditions from earlier proverbs and fables written long before in Sumeria, Bābil, Assyria and Hellas. People had been reading and retelling these tales for ages, and would continue to read and retell them for ages to come. It was this talent of his to exemplify wisdom (if we accept the story) that led to Aisopos being given his freedom.

As each tale was read, Younis questioned Junia and Julian about the meanings, the language and symbols, whether the message was useful for daily living, and what else could be learned. Did the tale that suggests "slow and steady wins the day" always work, or should it be interpreted as cautionary, a warning to be kept in mind for particular situations? What lessons could be learned as models for how to behave and interact with others, how to be a good person, or merely how to cope? They examined tales that interrogated various precepts: hard work and perseverance have rewards; one must not overestimate one's ability or importance; humility is better than excessive pride; kindness is preferable to using force; greed leads to adverse outcomes; it's easy to despise what lies beyond one's reach; don't give your enemies the tools for your own destruction; it's better to starve free than to be a fat slave. Did might truly make right? What other messages could be guessed from these simple stories? What practical philosophical morals balanced self-interest against societal good?

Julian asked how it was possible for a slave to be freed. Younis explained that the process was called manumission, a system whereby a slave could sometimes be liberated as a result of a master's or mistress's benevolence, as appreciation for the loyalty of an older slave, in recognition for an extraordinary act or, as in the case of Aisopos, in appreciation for some literary and artistic talent. More commonly, manumission was achieved by the slave making a payment.

"How can slaves pay when they don't have any money?" Junia inquired.

"Yes, most slaves don't have an income, especially those who labour in mines or row in galleys, the most strenuous work, and those who work chained together on farms, but sometimes slaves who work in households receive gifts of money that they can put together to make up the amount."

"Why don't you free yourself?" asked Julian.

"We can give you some of what our parents give us," added Junia.

"Well, it's a bit more complicated than that. It depends in part on your father and mother. But would I really want to stop being your tutor?" Junia and Julian laughed. "What else would I do here? And even if I wanted to do it myself, I don't like the idea of paying for my freedom."

"Why?"

"It was taken from me by force. No one paid me or my family for the loss of my freedom, nor did they pay for any of the others who were enslaved," said Younis, producing a nervous silence among his students.

To clarify, he told them part, but not all, of what he thought on the matter. He explained that the system, in order to appear benevolent, or even claim to be just, provided this opportunity for slaves to buy back their liberty, or allowed a sympathetic master or mistress to grant it. For most slaves, those chained as they laboured in mines and rowed in galleys, and for most farm slaves, such an outcome was almost impossible, and even if achieved, it would probably come too late to be of any practical use. It was true that in cities and on some estates, a loyal slave had ways to acquire and save money, which could come from any possession a master or mistress may give as *peculium*, or from the charity of guests, or from presents. He himself could easily save enough money to buy liberty in a few years. But how could he possibly enjoy it if acquired by these means? How could he be beholden to a master or his guests or, in this case, to his own students? When money was received in this way, he told them, he saw it as a curse that should not be kept. Giving such money to others was the only way to be rid of this curse.

A slave could also be manumitted as a reward for betraying others, or sometimes a slave buys another to replace him, a transaction called *servus vicarius*. It has sometimes happened that the masters, when faced by possible defeat in war, would manumit slaves to fight on their side, as Sparta did with their serfs the *heilotes*. Roma had done the same when in danger of being overcome by Haniba'al, manumitting some so that the empire could enslave others to replace them. Many difficulties were also likely to arise after manumission. Once no longer a slave, one had to find some means of support, and could fall into demeaning or corrupt service. A manumitted slave could resort to less than honourable professions, becoming not just a wily merchant, or a walker in the street, but maybe even a slave dealer. Younis did not want to mention that to walk the street meant more than being a beggar but possibly becoming a pimp, whether a *lemones* or a *lenae*, or a prostitute.

To himself, he concluded that freedom must be obtained by other means.

Chapter 4

With each passing month and year, the dilemma of selecting content for Junia and Julian's education grew more challenging for Younis. How would he introduce other required subjects without betraying the world he came from? The children were simply trying to learn the ways of the world and grow into young adulthood. For some adults he was a tool to be used for their own purposes with little thought of his own needs as a human being. He was determined to challenge this thinking as he started Junia and Julian on more readings in literature and history, and began their training in rhetoric, the latter being a prized and crucial skill for their personal development and public careers. Younis puzzled over how best to advance their learning in this situation. While the presumed objective was to prepare them for life with others in society and for the challenges of working in the empire, for him there was also the imperative to instill in them a sense of truth and insight into what drove the social and political order of the empire.

Younis wanted to familiarise them with the great epics, their heroes, adventures and themes. He did so by reading or sometimes having them read passages or narrate scenes in the style of theatrical performances that would stay in the memory. He would delve into the recesses of an ancient past shrouded in mystery to find and express what was still essential about human life and still relevant to their reality. He aimed to make them aware of the breadth of human experience, rather than only their own sense of pride in their nation and its militaristic values. He encouraged the duo to reflect and debate, posing subtle questions such as: "What should heroes be like today?" Younis wondered whether their parents entirely approved of this direction. It had to be done in ways that did not raise too much objection, but then why would they object to a more enlightened education, he said to himself? He did not choose to be naive.

As it happened, the first literary manuscript he found in the library was *Odysseia* by Omiros, from which he started to read the first lines: "Sing to me, Muse, of the man of twists and turns, the man of many devices, driven off course time and again, tell me how he wandered and was lost after he plundered the hallowed heights of Troia." Younis explained this opening, telling them about the ten-year war waged by the Hellenic cities to conquer the city of Troia, or Ilion, a thousand years before. This was a story told in another epic also written by Omiros, why the war was started, its main actors and heroes, and how Odysseus finally devised the wooden horse that allowed the Greeks hiding in it to enter and destroy the city. That is why this King of Ithaca was called the man of devices, a quality that some considered a defect, seeing him as a trickster or deceiver. As an aside, Younis asked Junia and Julian to consider why some writers in Roma disliked Odysseus, or Ulysses as they called him, influenced in their sentiments by the story that a refugee from the destruction of Ilion, Aeneas, had founded Roma.

Younis went on to recount Odysseus' travels back to his homeland, a voyage which lasted another ten years. His use of trickery in the conquest of Troia probably angered Poseidon, God of the seas, who brought on the storms that drove Odysseus to many lands. Poseidon's fury only intensified after Odysseus blinded his giant son Polyphemus. Odysseus passed through many trials and tribulations that tested his qualities of courage and perseverance. His loyalty to family and city was paramount and helped him to resist the temptation of the two goddesses Kalypso and Kirke, who had turned his men into swine. Kalypso imprisoned him on her island, promising him immortality, but he refused in favour of return to his city. With divine assistance from Athena and Zeus, he returned to Ithaca to take revenge, killing the greedy suitors who were circling his faithful wife, Penelope. In the plot devised upon his return, Odysseus hid himself as a beggar, a kind of slave. His first helper was Eumaios, an old slave (himself the owner of a slave), who sheltered him without knowing his identity, and who, reflecting on the dilapidated condition of Odysseus' old hound, delivered this line: "Zeus takes away half the value of a man the day he's taken and becomes a slave."

As a contest to reveal Odysseus, Athena convinced Penelope to announce that she would marry the man who could string the great bow of Odysseus and shoot an arrow through the rings of twelve axes. Younis tried to recreate this scene for them, using long twigs in lieu of the axes. Even after Odysseus slaughtered the suitors, Penelope was still unsure of the man as her husband. She slyly gave him another test, asking the maid to move the bed where he was to sleep. Odysseus explained that unless some gods come down to do it no one living was capable of moving that bed, and described how he made it: "An old long-branched trunk of an olive tree was growing in the yard. I built my bedroom round this olive tree, finished with well-set stones, and added a strong roof on it and close-fitting jointed doors. Then I cut back the leaves and branches, trimmed the trunk off, up from the root, cutting it into a straight line. Once the bedpost was complete, I bored out the entire piece with an augur, and carved out the rest of the bed until it was done." Only then was Penelope sure of his identity, as no one else knew of this. Only then did she rush, eyes filled with tears of joy, to kiss him and wrap her arms around to hold him close.

"That's so beautiful," Junia commented. "I mean the bed. How good it would be if we could do something like that here, to build with trees and stones."

"Using such woods was essential for people in ancient times when they worked to build structures for their needs. I'll tell you an older story about the wood of trees."

"We're all ears."

He started to recount the story of the first epic ever recorded. The story told of the travails of an ancient king of Urūk in Sumeria called Gilgāmeš, who ruled in distant days almost two thousand years before Omiros. Younis explained that Sumeria and Bābil were far away, a journey of many days from the place where he was born. It would take many weeks to get there from Sicilia, first by sea and then across harsh lands. It was among the first places, at the end of a river system, where people came together to start civilization thousands of years ago. Younis could not read from a manuscript as he did with Omiros, so he started re-telling his recollection of what was narrated to him as a youth in his home country, where young people sat around the fire to listen as an elder recited the tale. Younis stood up and delivered the first lines of the poem: "He who saw all, who was the foundation of the land, who knew everything, was wise in all matters, Gilgāmeš, who saw all, who was the foundation of the land, who knew everything, was wise in all matters." Gilgāmeš did not start out being that wise, or knowing everything, but he learned from his travails and adventures how to become a good leader. As part god, he was huge in size and stronger than other men. At first, he abused the people, beating youth and taking away young women on their wedding night. The people complained to the gods, who sent a man of equal strength to confront Gilgāmeš. His name was Enkidu, a wild man lured by a woman's temptation out of the wilderness where he lived in harmony with the untamed animals who came to his call.

"Why did the animals not run away from him?" asked Julian.

"What do people do with animals today? They either keep them in cages and pens, raise them for slaughter, or hunt the ones still in the wild. The beasts and other animals saw him as one of them, as one who did not hurt them, and so did not flee from him. But sensing danger the animals ran away after he left them and became what we call civilised."

Enkidu wrestled with Gilgāmeš for the sake of the people, but it turned out that the two were of almost equal strength. Instead, the two became inseparable friends and decided to go out together on adventures. As bosom friends they embarked on great exploits, each one revealing something about human life and its beginnings. Their first journey was to tame the Cedar Forest and take its wood. The forest was guarded by a creature called Humbaba and protected by the god Enlil. Enkidu warned Gilgāmeš that the journey should not be made, that killing Humbaba and getting the cedar wood would be an act against nature, and would anger some gods. But they still proceeded with the hunt. With assistance from the sun god Šamaš, who blinded Humbaba with his light and surrounded him with winds, Enkidu and Gilgāmeš succeeded in killing Humbaba and cutting the huge trees to take back with them.

"You mean Sol," Julian said.

"Yes, it's the same god, who was also called Helios in the myths of Hellas, and thousands of years before that the god Ra who was the highest god in in the land of Kemet or Miṣru, what is called Aígyptos in Greek and sometimes now Aegyptus in Latin."

"Why are countries called different names?" asked Junia, and Julian nodded.

"It's difficult to always know for sure," attempted Younis. "Names people call their land may change over time, or stay similar, depending on language or other developments. Other times, place names are changed by conquerors to suit their purpose. Also others looking at a place from a distance can give it a name in their language, or change the way it's pronounced. For example, looking at land between the two rivers where civilization developed and this story was written, the Greeks described it as Mesopotamia, which means that."

"You should tell us more about it later. But why do they kill Humbaba? He was there all alone protecting the trees," Junia asked.

"That's the conflict we are presented with as unavoidable. Nature has its own unity and harmony if it is left alone, as it should be whenever possible. Humbaba is fulfilling his task and duty to protect the cedar trees and nature's wholeness. But people want wood and other material to make what they need in their cities and their homes. Are humans, as another view holds, empowered to hold total dominion over the earth and to subdue its animals and plants to their will? How could they balance nature's well-being against their selfish desire to exploit its resources? In a way, we get one answer in what happens to Enkidu and Gilgāmeš later."

"What is cedar?" asked Julian.

"It's a special and valuable tree, with beautiful natural patterns like the olive tree. Unlike olive trees, cedars grow to a majestic size and are useful for extracting larger pieces of lumber. They grow in the mountains, and in forests not far from my home town. Their wood is durable and has a scent that repels insects, so it is perfect for building boats, large doors and special furniture."

Younis continued the tale. Upon their return, the two adventurers provoked the anger of another member of the pantheon. The warlike goddess of amorous love Ištar was overcome with passion for Gilgāmeš. But he rejected her advances because, as he told her, she had turned past lovers into animals. Feeling insulted, Ištar asked her father, Anu, to avenge her by sending the Bull of Heaven to punish him. Gilgāmeš and Enkidu wrestled with the bull and killed it. The gods met and decided that one of the two must die. They chose Enkidu, probably since as a previous wild man he was expected to urge Gilgāmeš to show mercy. As Enkidu fell ill and lay dying, he turned to curse the door made from the cedar wood. Gilgāmeš mourned Enkidu's death, sitting at his side for days, and refused to give him up for burial. He ripped his clothes and pulled at his hair. He circled Enkidu's body like a lioness after losing her cub. Younis recalled the tender lament that was still fresh in his mind despite hearing it narrated years earlier: "My friend, whom I loved so dear, who endured every danger by my side, my friend Enkidu, whom I loved so dear, who faced every peril by my side, the doom of mortals overtook him. Enkidu, my brother, who was the axe beside me, the sword in my belt, the shield before me, the strength of my hand, six days I wept for him and seven nights. I did not surrender his body for burial until a maggot dropped from his nostril."

"That's sad," said Junia. "Why did he do that for so long? It reminds me when my grandmother died. But her funeral happened the next day. They had her perfumed and covered in flowers, and hired mourners to weep for her."

"We are told that Gilgāmeš was in great sorrow, beyond all else that he had felt before. His very existence was shattered. He could not believe Enkidu was dead, and wanted to keep seeing him, until it became impossible. He gave him a great funeral and ordered a statue be made in his honour with a breast of lapis lazuli and body of gold. The whole country grieved for Enkidu, the people in the city, the farmers and herders, even the beasts and the deer, the rivers and mountains were in mourning."

Now fearing his own death, Gilgāmeš started out on another great quest in search of immortality. He wandered in the wilderness careless of his appearance, disheveled, shedding kingly garments and dressing in animal skins. He searched for his ancestor Utnapišti, who was saved from the Great Flood and granted immortality by the gods, in the hope that he could direct him as to how to gain eternal life. After dangerous treks through darkness and the waters of death, he reached his ancestor, only to be told that eternal life was impossible for him and for all other humans. Instead, Utnapišti advised him to put on his kingly garments again and return to normal life and constructive works for his city. Younis remembered how Utnapišti said it: "Humans are snapped off like reeds in a cane thicket. The handsome young man, the beautiful woman, all too soon Death will carry off in their prime. For when the gods created humanity, they made death its lot. So, make merry each day, dance and play music each night, fill your belly, wash your body and your head, gaze upon the child who holds your hand, and let your wife delight in your embrace. Such things are the only destiny for mortals." Though immortality is impossible, he is told about a miraculous plant that will revive his youth. He finds it but as he travels back it is snatched by a serpent that immediately sheds and renews its skin. Reconciled to his human fate, he returns to Urūk a wiser leader, builds fortification walls and temples, and attends to his people.

"It's a touching story. It makes me weep and feel happy at the same time. It's amazing something so beautiful was written so long ago," interjected Julian, and after a silence: "We have a wall here too."

"Yes, but what is the wall keeping inside it now?" Younis answered. "Walls meant more then than they do today. Now, walls act only to protect against attacks in order to keep people feel safe. Without walls in those most ancient times, civilization would not have been possible. They allowed people to develop within them, to domesticate animals and plants, to have agriculture and trade outside, to use nature and create industries, to build temples and adopt one god as a patron, to devise writing and numbers, to read the stars and create sciences, to invent. At the same time, all of this tells us now that something fundamental, what is natural, has been missed. People have lost the balance between wild nature and civilised settlement. It is a paradox. As we progress, we lose something too. The passage of time does not mean that people and nature are better off in every respect."

"Some of the same events happen in both stories," Junia said, reflecting on the two poems. "Both heroes travel to dangerous places, fight monsters that are blinded, and are tempted by a goddess who turns men into animals."

"It's good that you notice these similarities, though the meaning is somewhat different in each poem," replied Younis. "Both are punished by some gods and helped by others. Both have an opportunity to achieve immortality. It is possible that the similarities came from direct influence, or that this repetition simply reflects what we share in human experience across the ages."

Whenever he read to them, Younis would show them where the manuscript was stored in the library, in case they wanted to get back to read it later. His intention was to have them consider questions, now or later, about wilderness and civilization, which one is better, or whether the two could coexist. Was the hero merely a strong person who fights bravely for his country in an army, or one who was courageous but also had enduring qualities that captured the essence of the times and promoted actions and works that result in what was good for society? What kind of hero is needed now?

Before introducing Julian and Junia to rhetoric, Younis wanted to give them some background about philosophical principles and how they developed. What is available for us to read, he told them, emerged over a long time. The philosophers of Hellas and now the writers in Roma's world have built on what came before them. Greek philosophers did not hesitate to acknowledge their debt to Aígyptos, the land its people called Kemet and Miṣru, as a place of pilgrimage and a source of much wisdom developed by people there as they pondered life and death, and the maxims and morals we should live by. Pythagoras, one of the founders of philosophy in Hellas, visited Aígyptos, where he received much of his education. He borrowed the word *philosophy*, meaning love of wisdom or knowledge, from the thinkers of Kemet who had conceived it thousands of years before. *Humans perish, bodies turn into dust, but the writings of life and love of wisdom are remembered forever, more lasting than a well-built house or the stela of a temple.* Philosophers in Hellas saw Aígyptos as a source, a place of pilgrimage, and also paid homage to the debt owed to their predecessors in Sumeria, Bābil and lands farther east who started factual observation of the cosmos instead of mere made-up stories and mythological explanations. What issues concerned thinkers in examining the world around them? What is the purpose of human life? How does one find the truth? How do we achieve goodness? What form of government is best? How should human beings conduct themselves? What is the reasonable middle ground between the extremes of rashness and cowardice, revenge and surrender, right and wrong?

Aristoteles laid down important principles that others have employed and developed as tools for persuasion. He named these principles ethos, logos, and pathos. In each, particular devices are used as instruments to promote a point of view that is presumably closer to the truth, or at least more convincing. Younis supplied examples of public speeches by leaders and senators that contained rhetorical devices, to ask whether they provided truthful or valid arguments. As the days and months passed, he prepared them for exploring other topics of interest, which they were to argue by using question-answer methods, rhetorical tools and examples, topics such as the duties of parents, the obligations of children, the meaning of bravery, what happens after death, and whether all the gods actually exist.

During this time, unrest was brewing in the city as the result of an incident with two slaves who had escaped from the estate of Fulvius Damophilos in Enna and were caught by the *fugitivarii* the next day. As the pursuers closed in on the two, an escapee stabbed one of the *fugitivarii*, not fatally it turned out. Whether the stabbing decided their fate was not clear, but it was not unusual for Damophilos to decide to have the two executed in the square, an event that officials, citizens and most slaves were instructed to attend, including children. In this case, Junia and Julian became directly involved because their friend Perpetua, Damophilos' daughter, who was about their age, knew the two slaves. Perpetua was in a state of great agitation and distress, so when she saw them, she collapsed in tears. "Why kill them for this reason? Is it not normal for people to run away from such miserable conditions?" she pleaded, her words tumbling forth in sobbing bursts. "I know them as my friends."

Junia and Julian complained to their parents about the coming punishment and Perpetua's anguish. Antigenes and Cassia insisted with them that no person from the household would be allowed to attend the executions. Younis was distressed by the event and spoke to several people in the Damophilos mansion. They felt helpless and complained about this master's repeated cruelties. For Younis it seemed an opportune time, however difficult during this tragedy, to introduce a rhetorical discussion about slavery. His charges were growing up and he wanted them in particular to consider one question asked by philosophers, whether slavery was a natural state or an acquired condition. He even pretended to be neutral in the argument. He would usually appoint a different view for each of them to argue, in this case asking Junia to take the role of Aristoteles and Julian to pretend to be Zeno. Younis read passages from the works of the two philosophers. Aristoteles wrote that certain people are by nature slaves, basically not much different from domestic animals intended to service upright more worthy citizens. The citizen, Aristoteles maintained, must not live a mechanic or mercantile life, for such a life is ignoble and inimical to virtue. For citizens in the best state to discharge their duties they cannot be tillers of the soil, since leisure time is essential both for development of virtue and active participation in politics. Slaves, like women, children and barbarians, should accept for their own good the beneficial effects of living under the control and guidance of adult male citizens. Younis contrasted such beliefs with the views of Zeno, who was a compatriot of Younis though born in Kypros. For him humans were by nature free and rational, so the condition of forced physical bondage did not negate mental and spiritual freedom. It was even possible for a slave to become the spiritual model for his physical master. Zeno thought the condition of slavery was equally the fate of those who were greedy or thirsty for power or subject to low instincts, that everyone who was evil or lacks virtue was a slave to his passions while a good person, possessing virtue and wisdom, was free.

To add context to the argument, Younis gave them a historical overview of the practice of slavery. It was common in past empires, not just in Roma, to have a large number of slaves, which in places exceeded the citizen population. He told them of empires in the east, and also about Athênai where Aristoteles lived, and Sparta which had conquered surrounding regions and turned the inhabitants into serfs and servants, some called *heilotes*, to serve its military class. Although people thought of slaves in terms of markets where they are sold as property or gained as part of inheritance or through home-grown births, the primary source was conquest. This was the oldest and most frequently used method of supplying humans for servitude. As happened to many city states and nations, the conqueror intended to subject people to control requiring total obedience. This was in order to work in extracting valuable metals and riches, to plant the land for food, or to remove a competing threat to the conqueror's increase in wealth and power. Korinthos and Qart Ḥadašt were recent examples of splendid old cities destroyed by Roma for booty. Their art and wealth were plundered, most males killed and the rest, women, children and surviving men, sold into bondage. Under the laws of both Hellas and Roma, however, if one of their citizens fell into bondage during war, he or she was still naturally free and could regain liberty. Younis mentioned an example of goodness by rulers, like Kūruš, the one called Cyrus by Hellenes, who liberated slaves in some lands he conquered and who respected the customs of other nations. For that he was venerated by people, even by Hellenes and Macedonians, and by Alexandros himself, who ended up conquering his country two hundred years later. Though as a king his praises could have been overblown, Kūruš did what he did even when some other people were still using the authority of religious books or other excuses to enslave and disown people.

Junia and Julian struggled to absorb what Younis was telling them, understandably overwhelmed by the kind of information he had supplied about the empire and the world in which they lived. They asked questions and sought clarification. Junia in particular expressed surprise about the views of Aristoteles, since she had heard his name as a great philosopher of reason and ethics. Both agreed to engage in this argument, given they were living in a society that practiced keeping others in servile captivity. Was there merit in the views Aristoteles held?

For the sake of argument, though she herself did not sound very convinced, Junia posited the view that most slaves were uneducated and therefore incapable of making good decisions. Thus, they accepted their enslavement without much complaining, and should yield to the direction dictated by their more knowledgeable and powerful owners. Aristoteles would probably not have objected to the point made by Zeno that a free person can become a slave to low instincts or to money, but that should not negate the fact that citizens are in general more capable of leading society in the right direction, and so had duties that required freedom from physical work. We have a structure in society where some people have to be held below others in a gradation necessary for its proper operation. She added that Aristoteles was aware of living in a city where the existence of slaves was needed to do the hard menial tasks that citizens would otherwise have to expend, a kind of labour distribution, thus accepting the realities by which his society operated.

Julian began his rebuttal by giving examples of people he knew as slaves who acted reasonably while some children of landowners, even some adults, were quite rash and irrational in their behaviour. The ability to reason and deliberate was not a condition that necessarily resulted only from the availability or lack of education or the condition of slavery since some illiterate people could demonstrate wisdom and logical thinking. He then added:

"To say that some people, because of who they are, when caught do not become slaves and can be freed does not agree with what is done to others who are made slaves because they are captured. If people are enslaved by war in most cases, how could the condition of slavery be natural when the people captured were free before? This common method of acquiring slaves shows that slavery cannot be natural. It also cannot apply to children born to slaves, who have the right to want to be free at every opportunity. If slavery by conquest is not just or right, all other reasons given cannot be correct, and the word slave itself does not apply."

Even Junia had to admit that Julian's logic was more convincing. "That's not fair," Junia smiled, with feigned disappointment, now a maturing young woman of almost fourteen. "You gave an argument I could not possibly defeat."

Chapter 5

As the months wore on, a sense of emptiness grew deeper inside Younis. The joy in his task as tutor was only superficial. What Younis did, to try to develop just two children into ethical adults, was done with dedication merely to lessen the pain. Yet such pain could not be numbed by library manuscripts alone, however diligently he pursued their study, or by having his students argue the merits of slavery and learn a wide range of subjects. Imagination exiled, the past stolen, the future barren of any concrete promise, all seemed to require some other substitute and diversion. Not long before he had been free to roam with his imagination, to seek the limits of his ambition and to learn from those who were wiser than he. Now, he was required to acquiesce without a murmur of protest to a life where someone else could presume to chart his life's direction.

His attention was drawn to the garden, its surroundings and beyond, both for the flora and more so for the walls, stones and rocks. It was natural for him to accept the Great Goddess as a source of life and the fountain of fertile productivity, but he was also searching for alternatives in his fractured predicament for what society had imposed on him, in which he was now trapped. He looked at the landscapes he had experienced and tried to understand how people constructed meanings out of their environment throughout human experience. What meanings did people derive from the soil and its cover, whether a forested region or a barren desert, or a fertile river delta bordered by sand? What differentiates the visible elements of sand, sea, stone, rock, and plant in human perception? What was constructed in response to them? Deserts and seas have fundamental associations. In a sense, humans sprang from deserts and seas, whether real or metaphorical, since no structures or meanings existed at the outset. In reaction to primal blankness, people grew green bowers of protection, the verdure to avert barrenness, finding comfort in systems and mythologies. Stones are friable remnants, dead quarries of life, symbols of hardness and fragmentation. Rocks are inscrutable essence, the most ancient of objects, bare in a fundamental sense that transcends excrescence. In their bareness, the stubborn rocks stand out like gods waiting for potent meanings to emerge as creations. Against the desolation of desert beginnings or the comforting verdure of myths, Younis recognised a special affinity in the wild silent rocks as an essential source in which all were alike and equal. The cairns stood as monumental forms, and tints of colour in rock intimated veins of blood. What other ultimate meanings could be extracted from their brow of impenetrability?

When Antigenes saw him next he stopped him to say how pleased he and Cassia were with the children's progress and how much they enjoyed their lessons. He wanted Younis to know that the lessons and his efforts seemed to be creating a closer brother-sister bond between Junia and Julian. He had noticed the siblings working together to explain and clarify to each other what they had learned, and they were keen to demonstrate their understanding in their own words.

"I'm happy to know that," Younis said, as if what Antigenes told him was something he did not already know and expect. He then inquired about what was immediately on his mind.

"I hope you don't find it odd to ask. Sometimes I have free time. May I be allowed to work with stones and rocks in the garden when possible?"

"I have no objection," Antigenes answered, though visibly surprised. "You can do what you like with the stones. Nothing will happen to them. They are just stones."

Younis began collecting stones and rocks from the edges of the garden and amid the grasses outside the wall. He found a chisel and a hammer and claimed them as his tools. The estate's gardener showed him a supply of flat stone left from earlier work. Younis set about to build small terraces and retaining walls where he could and to improve planting spaces and irrigation conduits. Under one huge oak tree in particular, he built a bench of perfectly balanced rocks and around it a surface of pink, blue and purple hued flat stones in intricate patterns. His eyes could somehow always select stones that fitted together in perfect patterns. Julian would come out to watch him work, and even Junia sometimes expressed admiration. Their learning had bred a certain loyalty as months went by, a human bond between the children of a slaveholder and the slave. "May I carry this stone?" Julian would ask as he tried to help, and Younis would let him place the flat stones in predesigned locations and show him how to adjust them so as to fit with others.

On one of their garden walks, Antigenes and Cassia noticed the bench and flat surface area. "Well, we must admit that you have built what now is clear the garden always missed. You have outdone yourself with all this work. We are much pleased," Antigenes called out and paused, searching for the words.

"These are more than stones. They are works of art."

"I am not sure that was my intention," Younis replied, smiling.

It was not that he wanted to please anyone, not even himself. With every creation and product of his hand, in building the objects of his desire out of nature, he felt himself more fulfilled, no longer alienated from his own labour. It was a form of expression others perhaps did not expect, which in a way saved him from the shadowy monotony of slavery that was beginning to seep into his soul. The stones and rocks spoke to him, and all he needed to do was to arrange them so as to coax meaning from them. They too were more than they appeared to be. He sensed, without being able to explain how, that they took him back to the time and place that had raised him. In this labour, at least, he was not at the mercy of others. He felt freer and more in control than those who enslaved him.

It is not certain how much this labour prepared him for the strangeness that followed. It started with simple tricks he used to perform to amuse the children. Being alone and friendless at first, he found strength in the simple aspects of life and the natural world around him and expressed himself through new and almost instinctive discoveries. He drew on the vast expanse of time past as well as his new environment, remembering as a child hearing the prophecies of wise old people about food shortages and other misfortunes, and later his own youthful predictions about the weather or other events. Once, within earshot of Antigenes, on an impulse, he uttered the prediction that a two-year drought would destroy crops and spread hunger throughout the island, and in the first year of the drought Aetna would explode and reach Katane. Antigenes smiled indulgently, but then though he did not exactly believe it he still thought it wise to take precautions and ordered more grain and supplies than usual to be stored and placed strict control over water reservoirs. That the drought did come the following year, and with it the explosion of Aetna, made Antigenes look at Younis with a different eye—as a special person with more qualities than appeared at first, more useful than the diviners his countrymen consulted.

His abilities grew, without his willing them. At first, Younis was himself apprehensive. All of nature held magic within. He recalled his mother's many short proverbs, easily remembered—an encyclopedia of popular wisdom, family relations and social life, nature's lessons of morality, spiritual themes, all assembled in spells, sayings and riddles. Seasonal rituals were brought into the home with special medicinal plants harvested at different times, medicine that could relieve or cure diseases and nervous disorders with preparations of teas, juices, powders and poultices. Whether good or evil, boon or bane, glad tidings or tragic happenings, the coming of rain or the spread of a plague, he grew more and more attentive to nature's cycles and to the movement and activities of its creatures, the birds and small and large animals. With time he devised more unusual magical acts and pronounced more predictions, unaware of their source. Other slaves heard his prophecies and grew to rely upon them, even finding comfort in what Younis said about the future. Antigenes informed his closest friends about the predictions and magical acts, and one of them suggested out of curiosity that he should ask Younis to perform his feats for entertainment at dinner. It started with small dinners for a few guests and later regular performances on major occasions. His magical acts amused and puzzled Antigenes, Cassia and their guests, though some guests did not want to believe his magic to be real and thought of him as the usual mage who tricked people. But even expressions of disbelief were mixed with hesitant apprehension. Some resented the position of prominence that Younis had gained, the benefits this new role gave him in sharing a space with his superiors. They were especially uneasy about the power that his acts and predictions seemed to exert, and as alleged masters many were unwilling to accept that a mere slave could even accomplish such feats. Nor could these landowners understand that his visions were sourced in deep and mysterious beginnings.

Antigenes seemed to believe in him, as he once said to one of his closest friends, Etruscus: "This man has shown me that he is immersed in an invisible world. It is a realm to which we are not attentive, but to which he can connect. I lack understanding of his methods, but I do know that what he foretells often comes true. Our oracles give us riddles that we try to interpret to our benefit, which do not always turn out the way we want. The Sibylline Books are kept secret, the diviners only giving us observances to control our actions. They explain how to perform rites of expatiation and try to avoid calamities, but do not reveal the oracles themselves. Are they real or do we adapt them so as to believe in them?" Etruscus told him he had heard that the same means of divination were ancient, that these methods and means were used thousands of years before in areas where this man Younis had lived before being brought to them. Etruscus told Antigenes about those other miracles repeated by people who believed they had happened and gathered them into writings considered to be sacred, stories, perhaps some even less credible than what Younis did, about a stick turning into a snake, or the parting of a sea and a river, or the sun standing still for a battle to continue, or the raising of the dead, and various prophecies. Those powers possessed by someone like Younis may have derived from long-held beliefs in distant times. "Is it not possible, if we are to believe those wonders or other forms of divination, that Younis garnered powers fundamental in nature that people relied on before these times? Perhaps these powers emanate from a time and place to which we no longer hold connections here?"

"And what is it that makes one a nabi, a prophet, anyway? People are sometimes put into situations where foretelling the future, connecting to another world, accessing a supernatural realm, grows as an extension of their predicament. Even if some miracles seem in themselves unbelievable, a prophetic soul, a metaphysical power, the ability to see possibilities for a future event, may be part of human nature, arising from powerful natural sources that only a few come to master." Younis himself had this thought cross his mind. If only reassuring himself, he concluded that if the way to deal with his present reality was not to be one of destruction for him and for others, it had to be the path of astonishment.

Chapter 6

His eyes were trained to look there as a place of peace and solitude whenever he went out on his early morning walk. This time he noticed a human figure silhouetted against the giant rock on top of which rose the Temple of Demeter. In the half-darkness of early dawn, he was not sure that the figure was human until it moved. Who could it be? He scrambled down the hill and walked through the brush toward the rock.

As Younis approached, a deep, quiet voice emerged from the side of the rock: "I have heard of you. Others have told me about you. You must be Younis." The figure moved closer. Standing in front of him, he towered above Younis' average height, brawny with powerful visibly muscular arms and legs, in stark contrast with Younis' knobbly knees and hairy legs. He looked to be about the same age as Younis or a bit older, certainly not yet thirty. His dark somewhat curly hair was tied back with a narrow cloth band. His large brown eyes exuded an intelligence not yet dimmed by exhaustion or despair. A face with trimmed beard, a deep dimple on his chin, a small mole on the left side of his nose, and a scar above the left corner of his mouth, were all identifying features that would surely be given in descriptions to the *fugitivarii* if he ever escaped, Younis thought. The voice spoke in Greek though Younis detected a slight accent and noticed that his name was pronounced correctly.

"Peace be upon you. Who are you and where are you from?" Younis said, offering his hand.

"Peace onto you. My name is Nilos. I am one of the ploughmen. I come from Manbij."

"A countryman, it is good to know," replied Younis in Aramaic. "Manbij is not far from my hometown Afamia, perhaps two days by carriage to the north." Nilos acknowledged the Aramaic with an approving nod and smile. As he spoke, it became clear that he had lost some fluency after all the years away.

"I'm happy to hear you speak our language," Nilos attempted in Aramaic as he sat on a rock and motioned for Younis to sit next to him. "Let us talk. I have always expected us to meet."

They exchanged stories about how they had come to be in Enna. Nilos told Younis how he was taken captive by slave traders as a boy at the age of eight or nine and eventually sold to a dealer in Capua. As he grew up, his size and strength became noticeable, so he was placed for training in a gladiator school. The other gladiators started to call him Nilos, instead of his birth name Fadi, an adopted name he decided to keep as a memorial to that experience and the men who shared it with him.

"I will call you Nilos," said Younis. "Maybe you shall decide to be Fadi once more if we are ever free again."

Nilos had survived two fights before being resold and brought to Sicilia when the gladiator school closed about four years ago. Once in the Antigenes estate, Nilos was put to work as a ploughman, an obvious choice in view of his physique. Younis remembered from his readings that height was indeed one of the specifications for ploughmen. Agronomists theorised that it was less exhausting for a tall man to stand straight and rest his weight on the handle as he pushes. This quality along with a strong physique and a loud voice give him the ability to manoeuvre the plough and command the oxen. The writers also argued that superior strength alone was not sufficient as a qualification and must be combined with gentle guile if oxen were to obey the ploughman's instructions without recourse to the whip. If the ploughman was brutal, the animals would soon be worn out, difficult to handle, and would not survive as long.

"Is that where you got the scar, as a gladiator?"

"Not there," Nilos answered with a faint bitter smile. "That was given to me by an overseer when I was still a boy. He once jabbed at me in the face with a knife when he became angry at my disobedience."

"These overseers, though slaves themselves, can be crueler than some landowners."

"That's certainly the case with our overseer, though he does not dare to come near me."

"You mean Juba. He is one who goes far beyond what the landlord would permit. Antigenes is not a cruel man. In fact, he is sometimes inclined to kindness. I'm sure he hears about what Juba does though, but he chooses to say nothing. You and I are lucky in some ways, but there are other less fortunate ones who suffer constant cruelty, who labour and perish. I feel we are mere pebbles carried along by a raging river. The current deposits us where it may, and we lack control to effect even the smallest of changes. We must never forget what is done throughout the empire and in many estates here." Younis waited and then added, "The whole system allows all manner of abuse, seen and unseen, condoned and ignored."

"Yes, it sows cruelty from top to bottom."

"Self-righteousness and self-interest combine to drive it," started Younis again. "It all begins with the notion by those assuming higher status that they are superior to others and are entitled to use them as they want for their own profit."

"That's too much for me. One word sums it up. It is greed," added Nilos, relishing the opportunity to give vent to his thoughts. "What I find difficult to understand is how these people convince themselves and others that they are righteous in what they are doing."

Younis replied, attempting to explain. "Those who justify it like to speak about its benefits, even using religious inventions and political writings to argue that it is natural and decreed by the gods, that the wars and conquests that supply them with more slaves are just. Justifications blind them to any introspection. It's the same with others who sanction slavery in stories about patriarchs who owned slaves and who spoke of their own liberation even while they subjugated and disowned other nations, robbed them of land and freedom. These lords of Roma and those here in Sicily find deities and heavenly permissions, fabricate principles and excuses to sanction all the injustices and hide their own selfish purposes."

As a ploughman, Nilos spoke about the labours of farming, the produce that accrued to the landowners and the profits to the empire that sent them. He had other experiences in various parts of the empire which widened his perspective about the empire and the situation in which they were entrapped. Younis, on the other hand, elaborated with additional information gathered from his readings. How did Roma build its power and wealth? Conquest was the primary method. Those captured, after others were killed, became the means of exploitation for the conqueror to accumulate more wealth. In the mines, they toiled in chains to extract metals to make weapons and tools and fill coffers with silver and gold coins. In the galleys, they laboured while shackled to each other, rowing to transport troops and carry products and other slaves for trade. Throughout the peninsula, in Etruria, Bruttium, and other regions, senators and rich citizens of privilege owned large tracts and swallowed up the landholdings of small farmers. It has become more profitable to bring in the slaves acquired from wars to work the land than to have the land worked by peasantry. As the peninsula grew wealthy, the abuses moved to new provinces such as here in Sicilia. The appointed landlords won the right to assign *publicani* to collect taxes and produce, and these collectors always pocketed more than their share. To protect its interests and its bread basket, the empire had turned a blind eye to all the abuse. What could be expected from herders and farmers, who were not much better off than slaves, except alienation and hatred toward those who manufacture their poverty? When rations and clothing are withheld, the slaves had no recourse but to languish in hunger and cold, whereas many herdsmen who were left to fend for themselves turned to lawlessness and robbing travelers on the roads. Getting a cloak to cover one's body was reason enough to take a man's life.

"So here we are," said Younis to Nilos, "a ploughman and a tutor whose efforts are devoted to the benefit and progress of others."

It was almost full sunlight, and time for them to get back.

"You wake up early it seems. Let us meet here again."

"Yes, it would be good to speak more. Our waking up early is not what some landowners want us to do. They prefer those who sleep long because they think they can control them more easily. Those who are less scrupulous arrange for them to quarrel on purpose so as to keep them divided and powerless. We must make sure our people wake up."

"Let's hope the people are ready to come together. I should arrange for you to speak with some herders and farmers. There are two in particular I think you would like to meet. I will make sure that happens soon."

"May your days be blessed," added Nilos in farewell as they shook hands.

Younis thought about this serendipitous meeting with Nilos as he walked back to the mansion. Here was natural nobility abused. His various readings in politics and agronomy, though not always a consolation, only confirmed with more force what he was becoming aware of day after day in observing the world around him. The system under which they lived in the empire created the means to fortify itself and devised measures of how best to hold incessant control over others, including those surpassing in potential and positive human qualities. In time, greed and cruelty had brought about other kinds of slow destruction. Surely, the slaves who continued to be amassed and exploited for their labour, even the barbarians that Roma kept trying to subdue, would eventually overwhelm this empire. And what happens to the human soul in all this? Who was morally inferior, the *servus* whose will was abused, or the *dominus* who assumed superiority? Was it the *servus* who had no soul, being defined as completely under the *potestas* of the owner, without any rights? Or was it not the soul of the owner and society that were corrupted by placing other humans in permanent bondage? The claim of righteous injustice resulted in many wrongs that ended up corrupting the mind and disconnecting the spirit, turning the psyche to subterfuge. Mother Earth does not forget what we are and shows herself unfulfilled in mysterious ways. The powers that build can also destroy. What would happen if this world were turned upside down, if the sickened slave gained control over the sick master? Could that bring about a better existence, or would chaos ensue?

Chapter 7

On an early spring day, it became known that a new slave would be coming to the estate. It had been more than eight years since Younis was added to the household, so this event was greeted with particular curiosity. Tabiba, the chief cook, told everyone that a young woman had been bought by Antigenes through his connections in Akragas to replace his wife Cassia's aging handmaid. Like Tabiba, the new arrival was among survivors brought to the island after the destruction of Qart Ḥadašt.

Younis stood at a distance from others waiting for the carriage. As the young woman stepped out, Younis felt a throb of the heart run through his frame. Tall and slender, as she walked toward the quarters she moved with a slow gait, an undulating lightness that reminded him of a tender palm tree bending in the breeze. Her long dark brown hair was tied back with an embroidered kerchief, her eyes at a distance almost black, nose prominent and straight. Her top teeth protruded slightly, an imperfection remedied by her full lips when she smiled.

Tabiba raised her arms open and the newcomer bent down a bit to accept her embrace. "What do we call you?" Younis heard Tabiba asking in her language. "Elissar," answered the voice. Younis moved away, thinking, "The name harks back to memories of the city's glorious history, its first queen and stories about her, and all that happened afterwards. I want to know more from her about her journey here and all that led up to it."

Younis had read about the three wars between Qart Ḥadašt and Roma, the last one ending in the total destruction of Qart Ḥadašt about seven years ago. Cato, the one they called the Censor, whose title should have been Conspirator instead, had visited Qart Ḥadašt during the period of peace after the second war. His was a mission of hate not peace, the beginning of a plan to bring Qart Ḥadašt to its end. Cato marvelled grudgingly at the city's structures, its well-kept streets and the luxuries all around in it. Gardens of flowering trees and bushes formed backgrounds for nature's cascading bounty, and blended into well-planned buildings and brick- or stone-covered passageways and larger roads where carriages could pass. Beauty was everywhere, as intrinsic to the design of each structure as practical function. Despite the harsh conditions of the peace treaty, which it observed meticulously, Qart Ḥadašt had regained its prosperity. It looked more organised and richer than Roma. The queen of the seas was still alive. Now the mistress of the art of peace, its trade ships plied the Great Syrian Sea. Though it had abandoned war, its unexpectedly rapid revival bred fear, envy and spite, a destructive anger which Cato turned in his mind into an accusation of decadence and profligacy. In this most senators concurred, unhappy to concede that such inexplicable prosperity should exist outside Roma. Unwilling to accept what they could not control, they felt fearful and inadequate in the face of what the city had forged out of adversity. Upon his return, Cato advocated for its destruction. *"Ceterum autem censeo, Carthaginem esse delendam."* "Further, I consider that Carthage must be destroyed," the Conspirator ceaselessly repeated at the end of his speeches, even when the subject was not Qart Ḥadašt. The imperial economist did not worry as much about any real military threat from Qart Ḥadašt, or from the Seleukidon kings, or the Hellenic city states. He, Manius Glabrio and Scipio Asiaticus and others plotted together to ensure the extension of Roma's power through war and trade, to rein in or remove any nations on all sides of the sea that stood in the way of its control and wealth, and to pit nations against each other for its own advantage. Cato also applied this strategy to his slaves. He liked to keep them divided and in constant conflict. It is said that when they grew old and useless to him, he used conium to put them to sleep permanently.

To the greedy, everyone in the way of their greed is vice incarnate. Qart Ḥadašt was to be destroyed if Roma was to grow richer. The plan to do just that entered into motion in the year of Cato's death.

A casus belli was contrived in order to break the treaty and wage a final war of vengeance. Roma had a friendship treaty with Numidia, a client state next to Qart Ḥadašt. A pretext for war was fabricated by nudging the Numidian king, Masensen, called Massinissa by Roma's historians, to infiltrate the border. Woe to those puppet rulers who seemingly never learn to put aside their own interests and, rather than think of the larger good, instead serve empires wittingly when in the end even they lose and become the next target. In his younger days, this same Masensen served Scipio Africanus well in Roma's second war with Qart Ḥadašt, his timely help tipping the balance and resulting in the defeat of Qart Ḥadašt. He is the same Masensen who took as wife Ṣaphanbaʿal, Sophonisba as Roma called her, a noblewoman from Qart Ḥadašt, daughter of Azrubaʿal. She had asked him, as a man with whom she had bonds of origin, not to let her be paraded in Roma with her defeated ex-husband Syphax. After the marriage, when rebuked by Scipio, Masensen sent Ṣaphanbaʿal a vial of poison on a plate, an odd way to keep his promise and not anger his masters. It is reported that before drinking the poison she said: "I accept this wedding gift. It is not unwelcome, if he has found it impossible to give a better one. But tell him this: my death would have been more acceptable had my marriage not coincided with my funeral. I shall not be alive and a slave."

When Qart Ḥadašt repelled Numidian provocation, Roma labelled it an act of aggression, declaring a breach of the peace. Conditions upon conditions were demanded by Roma's senate, carefully designed to humiliate Qart Ḥadašt and encourage their refusal. Reduce the ships in your civilian navy, accepted. Hand over all your arms and munitions, accepted. Give Roma three hundred young nobles as hostages, accepted. Then a final condition that could not be accepted: vacate your city and move it ten miles inland. Abandoning what had been built over hundreds of years, giving up monuments of past glory, leaving dear homes, temples, and losing access to the sea: each and all were impossible. Qart Ḥadašt refused, and Roma waged the war it had so wanted to wage.

Elissar was well received in the mansion. Everyone enjoyed her company and recognised in her special qualities of respect and concern for others. She in turn conducted herself with quiet dignity and composure, always kind and helpful to fellow slaves when she was not serving her mistress. That made her adjustment easier, though she was not particularly close to anyone. She usually had a quiet smile on her face, but almost always there was a shadow of sadness as well, a duality similar to that of other slaves, though hers seemed more intense. Whenever Elissar and Younis passed each other, they exchanged a silent greeting, a nod of recognition. It was as if they knew there would be more opportunity for interaction between them. Within a few days of her arrival, Elissar made it a daily habit to go out into the garden in the afternoon, when her mistress took a nap, and chose to sit on the bench under the large oak tree, the bench Younis had made some years ago. She would sit motionless for almost an hour, staring into the distance. It was there that Younis finally decided to approach her. He walked to the bench and sat on the other side.

"My name is Younis."

"Yes, I know. I asked about your name. I was told you made this bench. My name is Elissar."

"I heard it. I hope I'm not upsetting your quiet time."

"No. I am happy we are speaking," she smiled.

"I come from Afamia."

"Afamia must be far away. How did you come to be here?"

"I was captured while at school. I will tell you more of my story later. I want to know what happened to your city, to the people and to you."

Elissar grew visibly restless, twirling her kerchief with her fingers.

"Tell me a little of yourself before so I know what brought you and what you do now."

"It's not a long story. I lived with my mother in Afamia, a famous city a day's journey from the coast. I was seventeen when I was taken by the king's men with other boys to be given as payment to Roma under the terms dictated in a long-ago peace treaty. I did not even have the chance to say goodbye to my mother. I was shipped to a place called Delos and then here to Sicilia where I was sold into this household as a tutor for the children. Now tell me how it all began for you."

"Yes, a peace treaty, I know about that," she said sardonically. "What's her name, your mother?"

"Maryam."

"What about your father?"

"I did not know my father. His name was Aqbar. He was killed in the war a month before my birth. I still think of my mother and her worries about my fate, and wonder what is happening to her."

"It must be a constant source of pain for her to not know, to be alone and not to have you with her. You must tell me more about Maryam and about what happened in your life here."

After a pause she continued, "I had a father and a mother. Our house stood perched on the rocks not far from a white sandy beach in a small town by the sea called Hippo Akra. One early summer afternoon, when I was about ten, as I walked barefoot at the edge of the waves picking up shells my uncle Aqbal came rushing down to tell me to come into the house. I was surprised to see him because he lived in Qart Ḥadašt and had visited only two weeks before to bid farewell to my father, Tabnit, who was departing on one of his ships with a cargo of olive oil, incense and ivory headed to a port which I remember he called Heraklion in Krētē. I do not know where he is now or what happened to him. My mother, Thubaba, had started to prepare two boxes for travel. She explained that we had to leave immediately, that war was coming our way and enemy ships were close. It was dangerous to remain in our house, and we must go to stay with my uncle."

"I had not been to Qart Ḥadašt since early childhood, so on approaching the city I was struck by its massive walls. Upon entering the gates, my amazement only increased. The streets were crowded but clean and lined with blocks of residences, some as high as four or five storeys. Long corridors between houses led into courtyards where as I passed I could see extensive laid out areas each with a water fountain in the centre and spaces to plant vegetation and even fruit trees. In one courtyard where I hesitated for a moment, I thought I saw a very small kitten perhaps crawling over a stone. It turned out to be a turtle, which of course was the living creature that each dwelling kept to ward off evil and bring long-lasting health. Huge structures rose past the residences and the shops. One large building, I was told, was the council meeting hall and another among the many temples the Temple of Tanīt, as I could see from her mysterious sign of protection carved into the wall at the entrance, a triangle with two branches raised like arms as if in prayer and on top of it a disc and a crescent. The city was abuzz with activity, people having come from the surrounding villages for protection within its walls, carriages with people and foods, and ships in the harbour bringing in more supplies and materials."

"My uncle Aqbal had been a member of the Sacred Band in his youth. The next day I saw him as he stood majestically wearing his long-unused battle gear, an old breast plate, long greaves, short-sword and dagger, a marvellously plumed bronze helmet and a huge round shield. Younger men more recently enlisted were less well equipped, since the city had been forced to hand over weapons and hostages to meet Roma's earlier demands. All the people joined to help with whatever preparations the commanders wanted. There was no time or effort to waste in the face of this great danger, no choice but to defend and resist. Women and children, I was with them, carried stones and bags of soil to buttress the walls. Women with the longest hair cut it to wind into bow strings. Every scrap of metal was melted down to make swords, even silver was sacrificed to make arrowheads. We all toiled endlessly, fearing the enslavement that would follow defeat more than death. It was difficult to do, but each day the city produced more weapons. It raised a mighty army and was able to stand strong for a long time."

"I heard the siege lasted for almost three years."

"Our army prevented the legions from entering the city and repelled all the attacks with skill and courage. Our ships supplied the city from the harbour during the first two years, but in the third they were blockaded. Then a day arrived with the darkest news. My uncle Aqbal came to us and asked his family and my mother and me to hide in the house and not leave it. He told us that the legions had taken the harbour and breached the city walls from that side. He said that each street was fortified, that people were already fighting in the streets. He embraced each one of us and left."

"What happened to you and the family?"

"What happened to us happened to everyone else," she said visibly finding it hard to recall too much. "We were in a house at the western city edge, far from the harbour, so it took several days for the legions to get there. Maybe the soldiers were satiated with the killing and the blood, the looting and burning that were reported to us by those who spread the news. The battle moved day by day from one street to the next, temple after temple and house after house. It reached the Temple of Ešmun, where the battle stalled. Our commander Azruba'al was holding there, joined by more than nine hundred soldiers who deserted from Roma's legions. Why they deserted is not known for sure. Some explained that they were recruits from Sicilia and other islands who could no longer accept to see the massacres or take part in the attack, while others said their allegiance to Roma was suspect and so they knew they were being used in the front as fodder to be killed first. Whatever the reason, they must have been men of honour and conscience. But the legion commanders circulated reports, reports we did not believe, that the men tried to negotiate for mercy and that Azruba'al surrendered. It is said in one of the many rumours that when his wife saw him surrender, she chided him, praised the enemy commander, and in despair threw herself and her two children into a fire. Then Azruba'al is reported to have been taken to Roma to be paraded and later allowed to live in a villa. It is even told that the commander of Roma's legions shed tears upon seeing the destruction, recalling the end of other great empires and cities, and thinking of what could happen to his own country as the fate of all things human. I cannot believe all such events actually occurred. We heard that all of our men and the nine hundred deserters fought to the last man. As we were taken out as slaves, tied together in groups, we saw the city engulfed in fires and totally plundered."

"The commander was Scipio Aemilianus," Younis remembered from one manuscript. "Roma in its infatuation with self-aggrandisement has made him into a great hero with stories about his tenderness of heart and his sense of pity for his victims, even though his actions were most cruel." After a brief but bitter silence, Younis asked: "What happened next?"

"What the soldiers did cannot be said. It is too much to remember. The older women, my mother with them, were taken away, and the very young kept separate. I begged the soldiers to let me go to her, but they did not allow even a quick parting embrace. I think all the time and wonder if I will ever know where she is now."

"This is the constant, ugly side of this empire, which shows no mercy in achieving its purposes. It quickly overbuilds areas it has wiped out with parks and large structures, hoping to hide its destruction, rather than building cities where people could learn to thrive in equality. What happened to your city was done in many other places. It was in the same year that Korinthos in Hellas was destroyed, its art and treasures plundered, its people killed or sold into slavery. Other than those who survived from Qart Ḥadašt, the people brought to Sicilia as slaves came from Korinthos, from Iberia, Macedonia, Akhaia, Thrace, Kilikia, and other regions all across the sea. Qart Ḥadašt had relations with other parts throughout the whole sea basin and all the islands. Here in Enna, the connections were deep and long-lasting, since the people were allies of Qart Ḥadašt and had relations with it that are still possible to see."

"How is that?"

"Think of the name Enna. The city has many springs and sits in the middle of Sicilia high on a mountain. What does that remind you of?"

"I don't know."

"Think of a word that means what describes such a location in our language."

"Oh yes, you mean *'ayn.*"

"Exactly, it's an eye in the middle of the island."

"That makes sense. I want to believe that to be so, unless it happens to be a coincidence."

"Maybe so, but the coincidence is strong," he smiled a bit. "This connection has a tragic turn to it too. Many cities on the island had cultural bonds with Qart Ḥadašt, as with Greece, not just political alliances. During the second war between Roma and Qart Ḥadašt, sixty-seven years before this last destruction, something terrible happened here in Enna. Out of fear Enna citizens would support Qart Ḥadašt, the infamous governor sent by Roma, his hateful name was Pinarius, tricked them to congregate and then ordered all of them killed. Pinarius called the people, citizens, magistrates and their families, to a meeting in the theatre. He started to speak to the assembly, having told his soldiers to wait for his toga signal. The ruse worked. Soldiers pounced from every direction, slashing and stabbing as they moved, while other soldiers blocked the exits and killed those who tried to hide or attempt escape. Death came by sword and spear or in the stampede as the uninjured fell on the wounded and the half living on the dead."

"It puzzles me still why Haniba'al did not finish off the war after his great victory at Cannae?" Younis continued. "Why did he refuse to take the advice of his generals to advance on Roma when its armies had collapsed? Was it too much strategy, or too much nobility? Did he perhaps hesitate to occupy Roma since, as he said, his purpose was to reverse past humiliation and regain the honour of Qart Ḥadašt in a new peace treaty? Did he believe it was enough to gain other cities in the peninsula as allies, as he did? Had he continued his march on Roma after defeating its legions at that time, perhaps the people massacred in Enna three years later, the people in Iberia at the hand of devious Galba sixty-six years later, and the people of Qart Ḥadašt and Korinthos seventy years later, would have been saved. It is sad to contemplate such vagaries of history, which one is at a loss to explain."

"Our Haniba'al accomplished great deeds, but he made a mistake or two. That is something to consider so that the past is not repeated in the present and future."

"Yes. I wonder how he met his end. It is difficult to trust any of the different accounts by historians. We know that, after his exile, he joined Seleucid King Antiochos and tried to help him in the fight against Roma, though the king seems not to have listened enough to his advice. Roma pursued Haniba'al there too, wanting to capture and humiliate the man who could have destroyed it but did not. He had to flee farther afield to Bithynia. We don't know for sure, but it is rumoured that realising he was about to be captured he took poison rather than allow his enemies to capture him in old age. But this, like other tales, is not always the truth of what may have happened."

"Is his place of burial known? A mausoleum should be built for our greatest man in a place close to where he may have died even if we cannot locate his grave."

"We should commemorate other events of our history as well, as a constant reminder to keep before us. Here in Enna, the horrors of what happened keep coming to my mind and never go away. I can still hear the screams of the people in that theatre, the tears sanded in their eyes, blood clotting their throats, shawls imprinted with skulls and heads, severed limbs scattered and multiplying in all directions, corpses gathering and rising into mounds that gained life with death. I imagine even the soldiers who slaughtered them being aghast in weariness and despair at what they had done, the memory of which would shadow them for the rest of their lives. We must erect memorials to the massacres so as not to forget."

Tears Elissar had held back for years welled up and fell down her cheeks like a torrent bursting through the cracks in rock after heavy rains. Younis stretched out and placed his hand on her shoulder. "I am sorry for bringing up such painful memories. We must make sure in what we do that they will never happen again."

Younis asked Elissar to meet him in the same garden spot the following evening, as it became usual for them to do. This first meeting, though sad, created an impregnable bond that grew stronger by the day. They were both mourning the loss of their families and their lands, but in their private thoughts they dared to dream of hopeful days for themselves and for those who had survived. Being one sea, it was as if the waves of both their shores finally joined here on the coast of Sicilia.

Chapter 8

Perpetua was the daughter of the richest man on the island, Fulvius Damophilos. By fourteen she already had several suitors in waiting, apparently unfazed by the fact that her parents were legendary for their cruelty toward their slaves, of which even other landowners disapproved strongly. Perpetua was unlike her father and mother in every respect, and it troubled her that some of her friends criticised her for their actions. It is strange indeed how goodness can surface in people raised by those adept at cruel abuses. Her father had slaves beaten and chained—and, on occasion, executed—for the slightest infraction. Her mother was quick to punish house slaves for any misstep. Perpetua could not prevent her father from ordering torture and executions in the field, but she tried her utmost to prevent maltreatment inside the mansion. One day, a maidservant broke an expensive mirror. When Megalis found out, her wrath was instant, and she was intent on meting out severe punishment. Perpetua, thinking quickly, convinced her that she had been admiring herself in the mirror and caused it to fall through her own carelessness. The slaves appreciated what Perpetua did, how she felt for them, and spoke of it to Younis.

Over the winter months, Perpetua was stricken with a strange disease. Her skin was pale and she lost all appetite. At night, the house servants could hear her talking loudly in her sleep, uttering words and names no one could recognise. By early spring, her illness had worsened, and her parents could not bear hearing her in agony as she slept. Megalis became convinced that her daughter was possessed by demons. They tried several traditional cures, and her father even took her to the priest of Asklepios, but to no avail. Though she was certainly disinclined to accept help from a slave, in time, after all else failed, Megalis asked her husband to inquire about the man known for his skills as a magus.

Younis was called into the library one morning, and was surprised to see Damophilos there. Younis stood in front of them as they sat together on the couch. Damophilos started by saying that he had seen what magic Younis could perform and could testify to his other abilities to communicate with the spirit world. He had also heard of his power to cure ailments, and was wondering if he could give him any medicine or one of his reputed concoctions to treat a person who is ill-disposed in the mind. At first Damophilos did not identify the person's relationship to him. When Antigenes pressed him to explain more, he admitted that his daughter Perpetua showed signs of disturbance in her sleep, and they had been told by some that she suffered from the sacred disease. Others claimed that she was possessed by evil spirits. They had tried more than one treatment, but her condition had only deteriorated. He asked Younis again to give him a potion for them to administer.

Younis could not say it to his face, but said these words to himself: *the evil resides in you and Megalis, Damophilos, not in that poor girl.* Younis then stated that while he had seen Perpetua once during the day a couple of weeks ago, he had not seen her at night when her condition worsened. He explained that each of his potions treated a specific ailment only and could not be administered without making sure of the cause. Younis cautioned that such a condition was not to be taken lightly, that it required careful examination in person. Damophilos was skeptical. Even as he spoke of his daughter, for whom he clearly wanted to find a remedy, he was still unwilling to fully admit that anyone, least of all a slave, could hold the answer to his daughter's difficulties. Despite his wealth, he was a man of the utmost ignorance who could neither trust anyone nor overcome his prejudices. He could not imagine how to begin to search for the source of her malady, to recognize the intense malaise pervading the mansion, or even suspect that the child was disturbed by what she witnessed both her parents' practice on men and women under their authority.

Upon urging by Antigenes, Damophilos finally conceded, but demanded assurances that the girl would come to no harm. Despite this insulting suggestion, Younis told him that he was willing to help Perpetua. Antigenes turned to Damophilos and reminded him of the magic that they had seen Younis perform, assuring him that he knew the medicines to be administered were all of the earth and could cause no harm. He reminded Damophilos that his daughter was obviously suffering and nothing could be worse than to leave her disease untreated. Younis added that he did not expect her ailment would require any medicines to be swallowed. Damophilos tried to dictate another condition, and said he would agree only if Megalis and her maid attended the treatment. Younis explained that for a cure to succeed his daughter had to be seen by him alone just before darkness. The presence of anyone else could spoil the treatment. Damophilos said he would consider all that and consult his wife. Later in the day he sent a messenger to Antigenes asking him to dispatch Younis to his mansion the following evening.

Younis brought special balms, a poultice of herbs, a silver amulet, a thin ring of copper, and a fear cup with letters and numbers engraved on it, a *baraka* bowl. When he entered Perpetua's room, he greeted her by name. She was still in her day dress, sitting at the edge of the bed. She looked up, her face pale, and smiled in recognition, obviously remembering their meeting. He reminded her of his name. "Yes, Younis," Perpetua said faintly as she stood up, "You gave me that name instead of the other way they call you. Junia and I talk about you." He told her why he was there, to help her have better thoughts and not worry as much, to find peace and learn to sleep well. He assured her it will not be a difficult process. He did not want to say anything to her about the other world he entered to purge souls, since he could face that world himself instead.

It was almost dark. He gave her the ring to wear on her left index finger, and asked her to lie down and close her eyes.

Into the bronze bowl he mixed in exact proportions a deep green ink of herbs, tamarisk, thyme, wild sage and selected reeds, finely ground raven feathers, shavings from a special metal, and the saliva and milk of a black cow. He spread a quantity of this paste over the entire width of her forehead, and placed the bowl with what remained firmly between her feet. He took up her soft hands and moved them onto her bosom. He pressed gently near her heart into which he was about to speak with three fingers of his right hand. His left hand cupped her head, propping it up slightly. He blew out the candle that was giving him light and intoned in a long-measured voice:

bysmk 'ny 'wsh hdyn qmy'h l htymha w lntrt' l hwrmy dwk bt n'rwy tythtm w tyntr b'zyqt dhtymyn bh'r w smyh mn sydy w mn dywe w mn lylyt w mn dnhys w mn dyny w mn zky' w mn ftkr' w mn mydm bs w mn lylyt byst' w mn mlwyt hstft' myhyh w sqf w trf' drdqy w drdqt w mrmysy w mrmyst' 'sb'yt 'lyky tymhw btrfs lyqlbyky bmwrnytyh dsqrwt jybwr slyt 'l sydy w l dywy w l lylyt byst' 'myn 'myn.

As he incanted, hot quivers ran throughout his bones, coming from his left hand. His head was flooded in heat. In the corner of his left eye, he noticed the bowl quaking and the ring glowing. From the sack he took out a kerchief dampened by the preceding night's dew and wiped the now dried preparation from her forehead. When Perpetua opened her eyes soon after, he saw a different light in them. He raised her head and slipped the twine onto which the amulet was strung around her neck. The amulet was made of two folds of silver, nine embossed squares on each side with letters carved inside each box and godly names on top, into which he had inserted a small hide with secret words, letters and numbers in Aramaic. He asked Perpetua to wear it and not take it off for a year. "It is for goodness to be your guide, to dispel the darkness hovering around your soul that others might bring," he told her. "I will come to see you hale and hearty tomorrow evening."

Chapter 9

L andowners and officials from as far as fifty miles away were invited to the convivium in the mansion of Pedanius Antigenes. The praetor Lucius Hypsaeus did not want to miss the celebration and made a special detour to Enna from Katane on his way to Akragas for a mission. This convivium offered more pleasures than the wine parties and symposia of the Hellenes and Etruscans: fabulous foods and wines, slave boys and girls, eunuchs, courtesans, musicians and entertainers, whose existence the powerful deemed to be sanctioned by some imagined god, who for those not privy to these privileges was a god of gluttony to appease the most secret of vitiated wants and desires. And it was here the guests had come to watch a performance by the man they call Eunus, slave of Antigenes.

In the mansion's *triclinium*, more than twenty guests were reclining around long tables on soft divans lined with cushions, skins and furs. It was late summer, a time of plenty. Tables were decked with meats, vegetables and fruits, each dripping with a sumptuous variety of dishes and delicacies. The usual and unusual jostled for the guests' attention—whole roasted lamb and pheasant, skewered wild boar and bear cutlets from the hunt the day before, roasted boa stuffed with soft-boiled crocodile eggs, pickled dolphin, cold fish soup with tiny live guppies swimming inside, honey-dipped baby dormice and sugared flamingo tongues, along with salad bowls, heaps of a new delicacy from the East called *oryza* topped with pine nuts, and an assortment of pistachios, walnuts, almonds, apples, grapes, dates, figs and pomegranates.

An hour on, the guests were busy in animated banter as they nibbled at the foods. Three slaves were carving some meats into morsels for nimble pickings, while two others waited with damp towels for any lord's or lady's fingers to be wiped. Other slaves scurried back and forth carrying amphorae of different designs containing aged wines from regions far and near: Iberia, Bruttium, Arcadia, Thrace, Macedon, Phrygia and Sicilia. "Hispania," a slave would call out, and the lord who wanted it raised their cup. Near the entrance, too early yet, a slave held a bucket, a towel swung over his shoulder, ready for the moment that a guest might need to empty his stomach.

The most powerful and richest men were seated with Antigenes at the centre couch. Hypsaeus and Antigenes were discussing matters of state, the situation in Sicilia and politics in Roma. Larcius Secundus sat to the left of Antigenes, bending to one side to affectionately stroke a boy seated on the floor next to him, running the fingers of his left hand through the boy's hair, down to the neck.

"He cost me more than four thousand denarii in the Saepta Julia, almost as much as a beautiful young girl, not to mention the taxes and bribes. When I go to the market in Roma, I usually avoid displays on the *catasta*. One can never be sure with slave dealers and their trickery, the depilatories made from tuna blood, gall and liver or other concoctions they use to make boys and girls and other slaves look younger and healthier, or hide their flaws. This one is no cheat. I had to go to the back of the shop and haggle with a senator who wanted him too. Well worth it, you can see, large beautiful eyes, light skin, long straight hair, most fair too, and full red lips," he said to Gaius Petronius at the edge of the next table.

"Here," Petronius proffered his cup to the boy.

Secundus raised his hand. "No. I always have him drink sweet wine mixed with hyacinth root powder. It does more than one thing and keeps him radiant and ready."

Secundus looked half-intoxicated already. He was turning over his emptied cup and examining the engraving on it, made in Hellas of high-quality silver and had relief decoration showing Orestes and Iphigenia, the children of Agamemnon and

Clytemnestra, as they wandered in the wilderness after their mother's murder. The cup used by Hypsaeus showed a fight in relief, with two gladiators in full armour. One had peacock plumes on his helmet, wielding a scimitar and defending with a tall oblong shield, while the other held high a round shield and a leaf-shaped sword in his right hand about to strike. The vessel in front of Antigenes was a large skyphos with horizontal and vertical thumb rings on the handles, covered in floral motifs and raised relief decoration of entwined acanthus tendrils, intricate flowers, snakes, lizards, snails and small birds.

Damophilos always insisted on having his favourite cup brought out for the occasion, a special work of art commissioned to be made in Campania by Etruscan artisans using silver melted from the spoils of Korinthos. It consisted of a thin-walled outside sheet with high relief scenes, an inner liner of sheet silver, a solid rim to make drinking and cleaning easier, a pair of handles, one of them with a horizontal thumb ring, and three feet soldered to the base. Embossed on one side is the figure of an older *erastes*, bearded and wreathed, reclining on a couch, while the *eromenos*, a beardless naked youth, lowers himself toward the *erastes* as he dangles on to a rope coming down from the ceiling. To the right, a door is cracked open enough for a young man or older boy, apparently a slave, to watch with a sly smirk on his face. In the background, there is a finely embroidered drape and a hanging kithara. On the other side of the cup, the *erastes*, or rather pederast, beardless and wearing a victory wreath is handling a boy on his knees in the process of adjusting him, his hand forcefully grasping the boy's thigh and his right leg prying apart the boy's legs. The boy looks to be about ten years old, his tender-skinned body half-twisted to expose his groin, which has somewhat undefined strokes for organs, and his face in profile carries a puzzled look, almost insentient. In the background, pipes hang over a suspended textile, with pieces of cloth neatly folded on top of a chest.

A middle-aged but lithe female dancer moved briskly in effort-less grace down the passage among the tables and stood in the cen-tre. Her arms waved and her hips twisted to the tune of a kithara, and from time to time she bent down, her long black hair trailing the ground. The floor on which she moved is an intricate mosaic. Its patterns of interlacing geometric shapes join each other in dizzying continuity. Each pattern starts with a circle in yellow, surrounded by another circle in white and grey, and from the third circle in brown, orange and rusty red snake off in four directions two overlapping swirls each that make four *vesica piscis*, the shape of a solar eclipse. The four forms do not exactly meet into a circle, the tapered ends almost touching. From the outer arches of each vesica piscis extend two overlapping swirls that come out to join the next adjoining pat-terns. The central design is framed by a double box of interlocking rectangles in black on white, and spaced within it are smaller rectan-gles containing triangular waves in brown, orange and grey.

Three walls in the hall had large painted panels. The two side paintings open up hunting scenes. On the left, two horsemen carry bows and arrows ready to shoot at several boars in the foreground, wild flowers springing up around the prey. To the right, a tiger and a leopard are attacking deer at a watering hole. The tiger has dug its teeth into the neck of one deer, which is bleeding, while the leopard is about to pounce on a smaller deer from behind. Featured in the central panel is a scene of Dionysian revelry, a contest between Pan and Eros. Ivy-crowned Dionysos, son of Zeus from Kadmos' human daughter Semelē, is seated in the background with Ariadne on one of his knees. This god of wine, vegetation and orgia, Bákkhos in Roma, still Dionysos in Sicilia, is himself shaped like a cluster of grapes, nodules sprouting all over him, his pet panther stretched next to him on the other side of Ariadne. Closer to the contest stands a bearded satyr, who has pointed ears and carries a pinecone-tipped rod. Near him are two cultic maenads with spotted snakes rolled up like hair pins on their heads. All of them are watching the expected wrestling match between Pan and Eros. Pan is bearded and has goat horns and legs, while Eros is a winged boy. The background is decked with grapevine leaves still holding clusters of black grapes, interwoven with small birds and other winged creatures.

A silence followed after the dancer and musicians withdrew, and then a loud tuba announced the main event.

Younis burst through the entrance into the hall, sparks flying about him from an invisible source. His long mass of coiled hair was disheveled, the nostrils of his large nose wide-open and vibrating, the bony nubs on his forehead bulging visibly, his muscular hairy legs exposed to above the knees. He juggled three sticks high into the ceiling. As he reached the centre of the hall, he paused, and out of his mouth spouted a long stream of fire straight ahead toward the tables, causing some guests to gasp and reel back in alarm. He bent his neck to horizontal position, his short-trimmed beard sticking out, spit out a long line of fire almost to touch the ceiling, and then circled the fire again to the middle.

Younis stood in the centre of the floor mosaic. He appeared to rise, the feet elevated more than one cubit above the chosen spot on the floor, his whole body inclined to the back as he stared down at the guests, whose eyes were raised to meet his. He gradually came back to the floor, holding one stick in his left hand and two in his right. He moved the sticks to his left hand and stretched out his arm to gaze at the sticks. The sticks that seemed solid appeared to become limp and malleable. With three fingers placed on top of the sticks he twisted them around each other until the three formed a single intertwined mass. He motioned and was handed an amphora into which he placed the twine, which visibly sprouted a green branch.

The guests applauded, more of them sitting up so the applause this time was louder, their disbelief transparent. They argued among themselves, wondering how this slave could possibly accomplish what they had witnessed: Was it real or a feat of illusion? The performance over, the music playing again, several guests asked Younis to join their table. Younis went to the end table where Cassia along with Calestrius Tiro, Fulvius Trimalcio, Gaius Dasumius and Claudius Etruscus and their wives were seated.

"We hear from our augurs that your magic is the result of tricks, Eunus. They say you place fuel in a nut or such container at the side of your mouth, blow out as you light a spark to make fire." Tiro smiled, apparently unsure what to think.

"Did they examine my mouth?" Younis replied aloud so the others could hear. "I am not an augur. What your augurs say only explains why they cannot do the same, why their predictions are useless and come true only by accident. After the last long drought I predicted, I told you when the rains would come. I foretold the plague in Morgantina. Aetna would explode as never seen before in our time, I said last year, and reach Katane, as it did. My divinations have come true. I cast demons out of many, old and young, among them Perpetua, daughter of Damophilos. He and others will vouch for that. I have made the sticks go liquid and buds appear. You saw how fire came out of my bowels, which the gods bring out through me."

"Last year, you predicted your goddess will make you king. That hasn't happened," Trimalcio interjected, to some laughter from the others.

"The time has not yet come," said Younis with half a smile.

"And pray, how will you treat your subjects as king?" Trimalcio followed.

"I will not be harsh. My rules will be based on justice and moderation. The laws will give land to small farmers to prosper and feed their families, and crafts made by the people will be recognised with due reward for their art and service. All people will be treated the same, one standard held up for everyone, and no one allowed to abuse another. It will not be easy to bring about, as we are novices in change. But change will come."

"That's a change for sure. I never heard you say this before," remarked Cassia.

"And how will you deal with us and the rest of the masters and mistresses then?" Etruscus asked lightly. Younis liked him, not only for his name but also because he treated his slaves fairly and kept them well supplied.

"Better than many now treat their slaves for sure. After all, they are lords who rule today, not used to work and pain," he said to laughter from some tables.

Hypsaeus, uncomfortable with such talk even if in jest, put on a serious expression. "Pray, Pedanius, how do you allow a slave to speak like this and not punish him?"

Antigenes was unsure how to answer out of respect, and conceded a bit of truth in what Hypsaeus said: "We humour him, my lord. He is a helpless creature. He speaks in good cheer, and the guests have a merry time dueling with him in words."

Etruscus took out his money bag, counted some coins and walked over to hand them to Younis. Toranius Flaccus, Claudius Acusilaus and Cornelius Cinna at the next table invited Younis to share tidbits from the delicacies in front of them. "Come, Eunus, take some food from my hand," said Cinna extending his palm. "And here are some sestertii for your pains," Flaccus offered, almost standing up. Calpurnius Fabatus, sitting at the next table, added more to what Flaccus gave in coins. "Remember these favours when you ascend to your throne," Longinus Castor rejoined, laughing, and dug into his money bag.

Younis laughed too. "Thank you for your kindnesses, your graces. Enjoy this time and have a good night." He gathered the offerings on a tray, moved to the centre, bowed, and rushed out of the hall. As he walked down the hallway, he handed the money and food to the first slave he met: "Take this. Share it equally with the others." He hastened to meet Elissar, who had promised to wait in the garden after bathing her mistress. Now his mind was filled with her. One thought stood out above the others: *how great she will be when she becomes my queen.*

Chapter 10

As he walked back to the mansion from his early morning watch, Younis recalled meeting Elissar in the garden after his performance at the convivium. It was a special evening, exactly one year since they took their vows on the bench he had built under the huge oak tree. He was sitting on the very same bench, his back to the mansion and the noisy festivities that continued there. Elissar crept up behind him, wrapped her arms around his shoulder and buried her face in his hair. He laughed a bit, took her left arm and brought her around toward him onto his lap. She was wearing a simple linen tunic with dark brown lining. Around her shoulders she carried the embroidered silken shawl her mother had given her before their separation.

"You smell sweet, my love." He put his lips to her neck and kissed it.

"Perhaps because I took a bath myself after I finished giving one to the mistress." She got off his lap, sat next to him and held his hand.

"Even without that you take me to another world, and I haven't drunk any wine."

"I heard people in the hall applauding. I heard from others that the lords were in amazement at your magic."

"I care little what they think, A few of them are kind, but most mock me and think I am tricking them, or take what I do lightly, as if it is done only for their enjoyment."

"Still, I hear others believe in your magic, are in awe of it. They treat you well after and give you rewards."

"I have no need of their rewards. My wish is to have the power to change their souls for the good, a fanciful imagining I know. Every time I see what happens to those in the mansions and fields, I do not care to be that lucky with such quick rewards. I cannot stop thinking about the cruelties inflicted by owners and overseers on all those men and women labouring in the farms and mansions, or worse those chained in mines and galleys, where few survive for more than a few years. Their suffering weighs on my shoulders as if I was taking it all on myself at once. It overwhelms me this feeling of being powerless to change it. It scrapes at my heart, brings the blood to my head. They live their lives, these lords, their wives and children, have their little joys, carry out their silly actions and go on with their lives of uncaring plenty. I see our people walking home at day's end with glazed eyes as if they already inhabit the kingdom of death— soulless, aimless, with no life ahead of them."

"I am sad to hear these heavy thoughts. We must try to help as much as we can until such a time that we can do more. How could their fate be much different unless it all changes and what was lost is restored? Let us do our best for them at this time, my love."

"You know that you are my life, the source of my happiness. I always think about you and wonder how our lives would be if we were free. Our situation is better than that of others, but not much better. We spoke about having a child or more. But what can we build seeing how things are? What future would be theirs if with their birth we only bring more slaves into this world?"

"Maybe it will all change, and we can have a child or more."

Younis started to untie a pouch attached to his belt.

"I have something for you."

From the pouch, he took took out a necklace—an oval-shaped pendant hanging on a double loop-in-loop chain. The deep blue lapis pendant, fitted into an intricately worked gold frame, had an embossed female head on one side. Younis turned it over and pointed out the letters carved into the lapis at the back.

"What does it say?" Elissar tried to read. "These are our letters but I can't make them out."

"See this one on the right is *alif,* the first letter, the one that started all letters, then the letter *lam,* going into the letters *ya* and *sīn*, this one with the teeth, another *alif*, and the last one is *ra*, which looks like a head."

"Oh, now I see my name. I never thought the letters would look so beautiful done like this together. It must have taken a long time to make."

She kissed him on the lower lip, and then gave him a deeper kiss. She placed the necklace around her neck and stood up to show him. Younis stood up too, took her hand, and they walked toward the arbour.

They agreed to meet early the next day. Elissar and her friend Lamia were to go to the farm stores to bring supplies for the kitchen. Younis did not have to go, but asked if he could escort them and help out with the heavy items. Antigenes and Cassia knew that Elissar and Younis were close and did not try to prevent their union. In fact, they were amenable, maybe because they sensed a special quality about it, as they recalled happy young love.

It was a hot day, and Elissar decided to start early as soon as Younis arrived from his walk. Lamia took charge of driving the empty cart and walked ahead down the hill to give Elissar and Younis space to talk. On earlier occasions, they all took the trip lightly and were more jovial. Sometimes Younis would force Elissar into the cart and push her fast until she started to scream. On this day, he appeared pensive and spoke little.

Cypresses lining the downhill path on both sides provided intermittent shade. At the bottom, vineyards stretched up the slope of another hill to the right of the road. A group of ten men were collecting the last grapes of the season, the best for the tables and the rest to make wine or vinegar. Men assigned to work in viticulture, like these men, were chosen to be short or medium in height. Two of them were chained together and shackled at the collar as well, as is done to wild animals, working in tandem low under the vines. Even from this distance one could read a large letter F, for *fugitivus*, imprinted on their foreheads. They had tried to escape and were lucky, in a sense, to be kept alive. Roma's law gives the owner the absolute right to execute escapees by a means of his choosing since they are thought to have run away with his property— their own bodies. They were saved from death in this case by the mercy of Antigenes, but not from punishment by his overseer. Some agronomists would recommend that, though the owner is compensated for the loss from the constant supply of war captives, execution is not always recommended. Troublesome slaves could instead be profitably used in viticulture since those who complained, misbehaved or ran away were often more dexterous and resourceful. One considered a good slave was not necessarily better than one classified as a bad slave if the latter was nimble and intelligent, experts said. Vineyard work did not require quick movement and occurs at low height, so those doing it could remain in chains while not unduly affecting output.

Younis could not help this thinking as he observed the slaves at work, having read two agronomical books in the Antigenes library during the last few months. To see the policies and practices elaborated in such detail made him realise the extent to which everything was planned and deliberate. The treatises explained how the system calculated each task for optimum effect, how the instruments of labour were to be used, how to keep the inarticulate and speechless instruments, like cattle and tools, in the best condition, and how to distribute the instruments endowed with speech, namely slaves, to do certain tasks that fit their physical and mental abilities. The books explained how to maximise output with minimum expense, how to breed passivity or inflict punishment, and how to reduce the talking instruments to their most basic needs and instincts in order to keep them under control. Ten was the number recommended for groups of slaves in farm work, preferably men from different regions for fear that if most speak the same language, they could communicate easily and agree to complain or cause trouble. It may be necessary to keep changing the formation of groups to discourage friendships.

With small groups it is easier to distinguish those who work hard from those who are slack and negligent. If scattered or in groups of more than ten, supervision becomes more difficult, since a slave might consider himself part of a crowd and try to get away with less effort. Imperial agronomists theorised that this system avoided the danger of a coherent group, while ensuring that the men worked more responsibly, and it readily identified those not pulling their weight and therefore worthy of punishment.

As Elissar, Lamia and Younis arrived to the level fields, they sighted a group of diggers and ploughmen preparing tracts after the last harvest and before the rains. They noticed Nilos driving an ox close to them at the edge of the field near the road. He stood much taller than all those around him in the field. They all paused, waved in salute. Younis and Elissar knew that Lamia and Nilos liked each other and were meeting in secret.

They rushed past the fields and reached the building where the harvests were stored. Attached to it is the small residence of the *vilicus* or overseer. Younis knocked on the door and called out "Juba." Juba came out and behind him the woman assigned to live with him, Marcella, ample bodied and clear-featured with dark straight hair cropped short. He was middle-aged of medium stature, with broad shoulders and stout, short legs. His beard was shaved and his eyes were too small for his large head, which, added to the effect of a wide nose, gave the impression that his face was almost flat. His posture betrayed the kind of confidence that comes from position rather than character.

Younis neither liked nor trusted Juba, whom he considered crafty and evasive. Overseers were chosen for their loyalty and experience, for their ability to delegate work effectively and keep slaves under control. Though Juba was almost illiterate, this was by no means considered always a disadvantage by agronomists and planners, who argued that a qualified overseer who could not read and write would still be a good candidate to supervise an estate as long as he had a first-rate memory. He could even bring his master more money since he was unable to cook up the figures so easily himself, and would be unlikely to want to get a literate slave to co-operate in cheating his master. Younis wondered who might have chosen Juba, or whether Antigenes himself had carefully considered these characteristics in deciding to appoint him as overseer.

Younis had other reasons to dislike Juba, more than just his enforcing punishments on fellow slaves that Antigenes did not directly prescribe or sanction as practices, about which he might have preferred to be kept in the dark. Juba acted with severity and even enjoyed selecting the cruelest possible *carnifex* to administer floggings, often using a *flagellum* with extra features, not a single whip but one with three strips tipped with metal to worsen the scourging. He discouraged any foreign customs and was meticulous about enforcing general directives to promote the rituals of Roma, as proof of his allegiance, although the gods professed by Roma as divine did not mean much to the slaves and some were considered quite ridiculous. Of most concern to Elissar and Younis was the way Juba treated Marcella. To secure an overseer's loyalty, a master allowed him to profit by giving him some livestock as his own and allocating a woman to cook for him and satisfy his sexual needs. Juba was known to be rough with Marcella and beat her frequently. It was also rumoured that Juba took young boys by trick or force to the edge of the forest, and allowed males to get together with female slaves for a payment, usually in any valuables or extra labour in lieu of money, as some prominent statesmen are known to have done, though none of them has been labelled as a pimp.

Marcella brought out an earthen jug of cool water for them to drink, and then walked back into the house with Elissar. Juba unlocked a large padlock and swung open the gate of the storehouse. Lamia read the list to him and Juba went about fetching twelve small canvas bags of lentils, beans, flour and other grains which he and Younis placed into the cart.

"We thank you for your help, Juba. Allow me to ask a favour of you."

"Yes of course, you are one to listen to."

"Will you treat Marcella well? She's a good woman and deserves to be taken care of."

"You can be assured that I treat her like a good wife should be treated," Juba answered.

On the way back to the mansion, Younis was driving the cart uphill, with Elissar and Lamia often offering or pretending to help by pushing him from the back. Younis stopped under the shade and turned to ask Elissar, "So what did you learn from Marcella?"

"Not much has changed. It is terrible. She tells me that the night before last she was not feeling well, but he wanted to have sex. She tried to explain, but he did not want to listen. He struck her on the face and had his way with her from the back."

"The brute, I will destroy his luck."

As they retraced their path among the fields and vineyards, Younis was pushing and thinking. *Work is done by feet that are chained by hands that are caned by muscles burst with whips by brows that are branded.* He was holding the cart back as they went downhill, his mind flooded with visions and premonitions of a seismic change to come. *Mechanical power against nature reaps unwholesome reward prosperity for the few brings not ease but arrogance and abuse what the land still produces by nature the precious metals the tributes coming in from conquered territories all make for more tenacious hanging on this efficiency destroys the spirit brings the worse in master and slave alike.*

Chapter 11

The mansion of Larcius Secundus was situated on a little hill to the west of the citadel. A massive rectangular structure with a large portico supported by twenty columns, it was built into the hill so its back gardens occupy the top of the hill and slope sharply into the valleys. Secundus had a smaller house in the city, as do other landowners who appreciated the protection and advantages of a pied-à-terre within city walls. In view of its unusual location, the mansion is fortified with a high wall in the front and a lower one in the back.

On this day, there were more guards on duty than usual, since many of Enna's landowners and officials were attending the banquet. Twenty-four slaves were in service at the mansion, fourteen males and ten females, several of them busily going back and forth between the banquet and the kitchens. A young man and woman standing in a store room were the exception, obviously uninvolved in the preparations, agitated and in distraught argument. The man sheathed the butcher knife he was holding into the woollen belt at the back under his tunic. As he swung around to go, the woman clutched his left hand.

"Don't go, Dariush. You know what will happen," she pleaded in a desperate voice. He pulled her toward him and hugged her.

"You are dearer to me than all else in life, Racilia. You are my wife, not by the law of our captors, but by the sacred vows we spoke to each other in the hollow of the old olive tree."

"I should not have told you."

"He owns us, punishes us at will, but has no right to abuse you in this way. How can I accept what he has done to you? It is more than injustice. Nothing is worse in humiliation to you and to me. His hands on you, I can smell his drunken sweat, the pig. I waited all afternoon for him to come back for the banquet. I know what I must do no matter what happens."

"Think of what they told us if anyone harms one of the land-lords. They will destroy us," Racilia pleaded. Dariush pulled his hand from her hold and moved outside the door, his eyes stone-willed, looking back.

"Don't stay here. No one will see you if you leave. Go to the cave and don't move from it. I'll find a way to get there. By heaven's favour we'll meet soon."

"Dariush," she cried after him as he ran into the courtyard toward the banquet hall and Secundus. She could do nothing. The situation had gone far beyond rational thinking, and it was impossible to hold back impulses or calculate consequences.

Dariush slowed his pace as he entered the banquet hall. He took deliberate steps toward the main table where Secundus and Cornelia were sitting. Slaves were moving about carrying jugs of wine and putting out more food dishes. No one noticed him at first. It was not unusual for Dariush to serve the master or other tables, though this time he was carrying nothing as he moved behind the table. Dariush got closer. Secundus turned toward him, noticing him with irritation. When Dariush stopped close behind him, Secundus stood up in instinctual annoyance. "Dis Pater, what in the . . ." he began. In one quick motion, Dariush pulled the knife and thrust it into Secundus' lower abdomen, cutting down to the groin. He left the knife inside, turned and ran toward the entrance. The hall exploded in cries and shouts of anger and panic. Secundus held on to the table for a moment, with a look of surprise on his face. His bowels spilled forth as he hit the edge of the table and collapsed into a pool of his own blood.

Dariush exited the back entrance into the path, with three guards in hot pursuit. He turned left from the path toward the edge of the orchard. If he could jump the wall into the brush, the oncoming darkness would help him get away down the hills. He was only a few feet from the wall when one of the guards threw a javelin, which felled him. The guards reached Dariush lying down on his side, his back against a large stone. When he turned his head to look up toward them a sword came down, splitting his skull open.

Racilia heard the commotion, and knew she must do what Dariush had told her to do. She went outside the building and hid at the back of the kitchen. She noticed the light of torches and heard guards going back and forth on the cobble walkway. To cross the orchard, she moved from one juniper hedge to the next and hid behind trees until she reached the stone wall, climbed it and ran down the hills.

Racilia could read her way to the cave by the moonlight and stars. It was a familiar landscape she had walked before many times in spring and summer, over a rough terrain of stone, rock and dry bush. In darkness she could not always find the easy trails they took by daylight or avoid stepping on the stones and brush. By this time of year, the thistles had dried completely and thorns scratched the sides of her legs. She stumbled and fell many times, but quickly raised herself up to continue on.

Once she entered through the small opening covered by bushes, the cave expanded into a large chamber and continued for more than a hundred metres to another opening. The inside was stocked with water, dry items and blankets that Racilia and Dariush and close friends had left there. She drank some water and covered herself with a blanket to rest, and tried to sleep. The minutes moved by slowly. After a few hours, she started from her half-sleep, and could no longer wait, restless to find out why Dariush had not appeared. She decided to go back to the mansion to try to find out.

It was totally dark, the moonlight gone. She stumbled as she stepped on stones, thorns and brambles, trying to run faster in fear of wild dogs howling in the distance. It took more than an hour longer to see the lights from the mansion. It was not yet dawn. As she climbed back into the orchard, she heard the distant voices of the guards. She knew she must not show herself. She crouched behind a hedge to listen.

Chapter 12

Dawn was breaking, the horizon bright, almost time for Younis to get back to the mansion. Out of his long morning recollections came an uneasy feeling that grew into a foreboding that something large and unforeseen was about to happen. What it would be except a great change was uncertain. Would it lead to good or to evil? Beyond the edges of silence and in the shadows where the sun's rays had not yet fully dissipated the night's darkness, he stood up to walk.

"Younis," a woman's voice barely whispered. As Racilia's frail figure approached, Younis could see her face in the half light of dawn. It was contorted by fear and dread, making her at first almost unrecognizable as she drew closer. She was haggard and tearful, veiled in sadness, her legs and arms scratched and bleeding. Something terrible had happened.

"Dariush is no more. Secundus is dead. Dariush killed him and the guards killed Dariush. What must we do?"

His brow and his lips tightened. Younis moved closer and brought Racilia toward him, holding her small head to his chest as she cried. She was about twenty-five, a skinny woman, bony and short, with hazel eyes and dark brown hair cut short. Younis had always held a special affection for Racilia ever since she told him what happened to her as a girl. After seeing her house burn, her father killed and her siblings taken, she was pulled away from her mother and brought to the island.

"I went to the cave as Dariush told me and waited until after midnight, but Dariush did not come," she said, struggling to bring out the words through breathlessness and tears. "Then I went back in the dark until I reached the mansion walls. There was still a lot of movement, but I knew where I could hide. I heard voices from various directions, the frantic utterances of my friends and the guards shouting, furious about what Dariush had done on their watch. One guard described how they finally caught up with Dariush, bragging about it, I had to hold my mouth shut to avoid being heard. I could gather that they were beginning to round up some of our people for punishment, anyone close to Dariush or suspected of not preventing the murder. They must be looking for me too. You know what will happen today and tomorrow. I came here because I remember this is the place to find you early in the morning."

Younis held her hand, and they moved to sit at the edge of a rock.

"What made him do it?"

"It was my fault. I don't know why I told him. You know how he was in rage whenever he saw an injustice in this unending hell. Secundus came in the night, slipped under my cover and woke me as he tried to pull up my gown. He was drunk. I could smell him, sour and dirty. I screamed for help but he slammed his hand onto my mouth, dragged me into an empty room next to ours. One of the women, Balya, woke up too and saw what he was doing. I tried to wash his dirt away. I was frightened and disgusted and could not sleep for the rest of the night. When I saw Dariush later in the morning I made the mistake of telling him when he noticed my condition and asked. His pain was unbearable and I could see that his rage would not be quiet. He immediately went out to try to find Secundus, despite my pleas. Secundus was out on one of his hunting trips, a strange contradiction to what he had done to me a few hours before, so Dariush waited until the evening, his anger only growing. At first, I thought he would only confront him, but then I saw the knife and tried to stop him. With the knife hidden under his tunic he headed off toward the dining hall where all the guests were eating. That was the last I saw of him." She stopped and burst into tears. "If I had kept silent, he would be with us now."

"Don't blame yourself. You did what seemed in the sorrow of the moment the right thing by telling him. What happened, what he did, was fated to happen."

"You know they will kill them, the servants who were in the dining hall and any others they suspect. Everything will change. It will never be the same."

"You are right. It will never be the same. We cannot stop what is to follow." Younis paused. "It is already light. Go back to the cave. Wait until I send someone with news. Don't come out for any reason. You will be safe there for now. I will have food brought to you later in the morning."

"I will do as you say," Racilia stood up. Younis held her hand, however little comfort he could provide, and walked her to the end of the path. As she moved away, he waved each time she looked back. After she disappeared, he went back to stand on the silent rock, looked south and east, and said to himself the only thought that now filled his mind, almost aloud: *Has the moment come at last?*

Chapter 13

The murder of Secundus and other events of the previous evening had little effect on the mood of the city's citizens or its landowners, as he was generally unpopular. Yet the law was law. Several slaves in the Secundus household would have to face punishment, as was the custom. Whenever a master or mistress was harmed, even accidentally and inadvertently, some perceived culprits would have to be punished. What was the source of the spite that emerged from the souls of some of these masters? Most aberrant was when they whimsically ordered brutal punishment for trivial infractions or perceived inadequacies, often causing permanent handicap, even death. If food was not prepared to taste or not served properly, the slave could be beaten. Woe be unto a slave if a temperamental master or mistress were not heard right away when he or she called, or if perchance the slave would dare to hiccup, belch or sneeze, or, even more unforgiveably, produce an accidental fart in their owner's presence. Once a slave got old, an inhumane master could decide to save themselves the expense of feeding an invalid, and order the usual dose of *conium maculatum* in seed or root. From one of the outlying mansions came reports that an angry master had stabbed at a slave with his stylus, gouging out his eye. The master may have felt sorry later to see the horrible damage, but what remedy was there once the deed was done? How telling that a tool of learning should become a weapon of abuse as mighty in harm as a sword. Another slave who dropped and broke an expensive crystal cup was beaten and whipped so severely that he could not move for a month and was permanently handicapped. But most egregious was what Damophilos did in one of his outlying mansions. A slave was accused of burning a grain storage shed, though others said he had done nothing wrong. Damophilos had a special pool in that mansion filled with huge lampreys which he kept starved on purpose. He was so upset with the financial loss, which he estimated to be worth more than a slave's life, that he ordered the man to be tied up and thrown to the lampreys.

Murder had yet more drastic consequences. Should a master be killed, a much feared though rare occurrence, the slaves in his mansion were questioned and those assumed to have been responsible for not preventing the death, even if it was an accident, or thought to have been in any way complicit or silent, were put to death. In this case, all the suspects were rounded up—those, according to the rule, within earshot, whatever the distance might mean, in this case four men and two women serving in the immediate proximity, including the woman who witnessed the rape. With Cornelia's approval, they were arrested and tortured to find out if they suspected or knew anything that could somehow have prevented the murder. Racilia was named as one to be arrested, so the *fugitivarii* were out hunting for her.

The men were to be crucified at noon in the square, and the women thrown off the cliff. This was a spectacle meant for all to watch, as instruction for the slaves and entertainment for the powerful. Landowners, citizens and officials were invited to attend and all slaves, young and old, were ordered to be present, except the few asked to stay behind for essential duties. Though the slaves knew about the law and were reminded of it by overseers, to witness these executions and their preparation first-hand generated a mixture of unresolved emotions: helplessness, vague culpability, and silent certainty of its injustice. How would any god allow such an atrocity? Why not punish only the person responsible? In quiet moments now and then when it was possible to remove oneself from the terror that ruled the city, a man, a woman, an elder or even a child would question the inefficacy of the gods of justice. For most in the Secundus estate and for others who knew those being executed, there was the immediacy of pain and apprehension, and grief for the loss of a friend or compatriot. Still, a few could not help questioning what Dariush had done, thinking of how what happened would complicate their lives by making the masters even more stern and suspicious. Yet fear reverberated even among some masters and those who carried out their instructions. Somehow the killing of Secundus while his guests were enjoying themselves at the banquet seemed to implicate them in the ugly outcome, causing fearful forebodings of an uncertain future that was seeping invisibly into their midst.

Secundus was known to be as cruel and perverse as Damophilos, and was almost as rich. Unlike other landowners and officers, these two were not content just to have their secret little aberrations satisfied in discrete ways. They both were gripped by a need to be noticed, to be the centre of attention, and to be talked about, and so they publicised their actions far too much. It was as if the publicity itself gave them additional pleasure. They forced boys and girls to have sex, it was reported, withheld basic necessities, and left other slaves in the fields without adequate clothing in cold weather. They often had their slaves flogged for trivial reasons, used branding and chaining as punishment too frequently, throwing some into dungeons, and for those accused of extreme disobedience or attempted escape put on sham trials resulting often in execution.

Damophilos, who owned large tracts of farmland for cultivation and pasture around Enna and in other parts of Sicilia, had influential connections in Roma and was skilled at ensuring the appointment of *publicani* who served his interests. He went about the countryside surveying his domain accompanied by a retinue of expensive horses and a paramilitary escort. In Enna and at his country mansions, he was keen to display his wealth by showing off expensive carpets and all manner of goldware and silverware. His banquets were designed to make him look like an all-powerful king. Megalis was almost as arrogant as her husband. She took pleasure in brutalising her maids, ordering beatings and withholding food and drink for long periods. People dared only speak of their abuses in whispers for fear of the influence Damophilos wielded and his ability to affect decisions by officials. Except for a select few to whom particular privileges were given for a purpose, the slaves hated the couple, and could not think of any fate worse than being in their service.

Damophilos decided not to watch the executions this time. He was likely to decide on others of his own the next day. Accompanied by an entourage of boys and eunuchs, and several guards, he sped off to one of his estates about three hours by carriage from Enna. Two slaves arrested by the *fugitivarii* after attempting escape were to be tried the next day. He had told Secundus at the convivium that he was inclined to execute them, and though he could instead brand and chain them, he wanted to put a stop to such attempts and general acts of disobedience. He was going to pick a method other than crucifixion or decapitation, which in this case he thought would be more effective, like having the victims fed to the beasts and their remains cremated.

Dariush's body was already hanging on a central crucifix with two empty crucifixes lying flat on the ground on each side as the four men were brought to the square chained and gagged. One by one their arms were stretched out on each crucifix and tied at the wrist and feet before the chains were removed. Two soldiers held each man, struggling and squirming, and inserted the spike jutting out from the *sedile* into his anus, to prop up the body weight for the duration. A muscular soldier approached carrying a long hammer and swung down to strike the shins one at a time as the men screamed or cursed through the gag. The blow that broke the first shin was usually enough for the man to faint, before the second shin was struck. One by one he went down the row of men on the flat crucifixes. Another three soldiers moved behind him, tied the arms and the feet more tightly, removed the gag, and raised each crucifix to a vertical position. The men recovered consciousness later, but it did not take long for two of them to collapse again, having lost blood from burst veins. On average, it would take about four or five hours for someone of average built to expire completely, sometimes more than a day for a strong person. Almost in an act of mercy (still some enjoyed watching the agonised twists and groans, which their brutalised inner spirit rationalised as deserved punishment), after about four hours, the soldiers thrust a long spear into each rib cage toward the heart to make sure of death.

After the crucifixes were raised, three soldiers took the two women with hands tied down the slope toward the infamous cliff. The women kept turning their heads, sobbing, as they searched to see anyone they knew as a friend or relative. The crowd stayed well behind as they were taken to the cliff. One by one, they were pushed over the edge.

All was finished by midday. The slaves were expected to return to their work, as though nothing unusual had happened, while some citizens and landowners stayed behind to watch the final agonies on the crucifixes. Younis and Elissar, with several others, took an alley that led toward the Antigenes mansion. At the first turn, they were met by a group of about thirty from the Damophilos and Secundus estates. An overseer from the Damophilos estate by the name of Hermon was a notable presence. He approached Younis.

"May we walk ahead and speak in private?"

"All these people with me are trusted friends. You can speak in front of them," Younis replied.

"We have just met and talked. We have decided with one voice that such outrages against innocent people must stop. We are all here of one mind and can no longer accept these abuses. Today's executions have intensified beyond all else the urgency of our situation as well as our shame, more than fear. The trial by Damophilos tomorrow, like others before it, will be a parody, the outcome pre-determined. We believe in your powers and want to know whether the gods would favour our action. Will you join us? These people are beyond despair. They would rather die than remain like this and see their loved ones being killed one by one, today and tomorrow. More men and women are ready to embrace our cause."

Racilia and Dariush came to mind. They too had reached a point beyond despair. Younis had been receiving news of other slaves as well as farmers and herders who were disaffected in different ways, waiting for the moment to break their chains, not only in Enna but elsewhere across the island. After a long silence, Younis spoke:

"You men and women are many and you speak your mind with one voice. You are seeking freedom. I will join you. The gods have talked to me in visions over the past days and weeks. Only last night our Great Mother appeared and told me that the moment has arrived and that our uprising would succeed. But if we are to act, we must act with measured haste. We must make sure. The day has already reached its half. Damophilos is gone for the day, others are with him, and the soldiers are busy in the square. None of you here who heard this will leave to go back to your places, except the women and one man for each mansion to make sure we are not missed too soon. We shall go outside the city to the Valley of Persephone. It will not take long to reach it. There we will speak more openly in assembly and decide how best to proceed. On the way there, we will ask the herdsmen and farmers to join us. We will ensure that what this bloodshed has awakened will never fall back asleep."

Chapter 14

The harvest in the valley had been bounteous that year, and most rewarding at the edges of the forest and in fields surrounding Lake Pergusa. In the stretches between Enna and this valley, some forest trees had been cut down for firewood, small sheds and fencing. In their place, farmers had planted barley, wheat and cereals. On higher ground they cultivated grape vines, while toward the lake several pomegranate orchards. This was the sacred ground trodden by Persephone and her mother Demeter. In spring, anemones carpeted stretches of the land, before making way for wild asters, pansies, marigold, mandrake, and herbs, tall and low-lying grasses, sweet thyme and sage that still grew in the stony spaces close to the rocks and the forest. Most of the pomegranates had been harvested, and on the trees not yet all picked off some fruits had split open, displaying their ripe red seeds.

More than two hundred men had assembled in the valley. Among them were trusted farmers and herders who were asked to join on the way. Younis decided to hold the meeting on a rock platform adjacent to a pomegranate orchard, as it was lined on one side by a terrace wall and stepped toward the front to provide natural rows of seats.

Nilos stood with his back against the terrace and spoke to the hushed gathering:

"Friends, we meet on these sacred grounds to discuss a matter of great urgency. I do not need to tell you what has happened and in what condition we have been. You are here because all of you have lived the dire situation and know it well. We are here because we have to decide what must be done. I only say what I think and do what I believe is necessary. We need someone to guide our actions toward one end. No person is more able to do that with success than Younis. He can be trusted to point out the path. He has the ways of healing magic and knows what the gods want and what the gods permit."

"I agree with all my heart. I have already called upon Younis to tell us whether the gods would look upon our action with favour," said Hermon.

"All the farmers here know Younis and believe in his desire for our good," Manus stood up to say.

"The herders join their voices with all the others here. We trust Younis to tell us," Munim rejoined.

In his right hand, Younis carried a short chestnut cane he had made, knotted and smooth, its head knobbed into a ball with carved circular studs. He walked up to the terrace, placed the cane on the stone wall and turned to speak.

"In truth I tell you that the gods have spoken. They have told me that we will overcome our enemies. Our ancestors and the goddesses of these fields foretell our certain success. I say to you that to be here and to talk about what to do is to hold our lives in our own hands. There is no turning back. We must be resolute and strong in action. The executions today, what happened to Dariush and Racilia, what Damophilos has done and will do, the past, the present, and a hopeless future, all of these leave us no choice but to act as one and at once. You who are with us, you who work the land and herd the goats and sheep and get almost nothing in return, you have already had the *publicani* take away the good harvest of this year and the best animals they want for their lords and for themselves, leaving you and your families with little to eat. Have you enough grain to mill for the winter months? Do you have enough milk left from the udders to make your cheese and enough skins from the slaughter to cover yourselves for warmth? Our enemies are treacherous and greedy and will stop at nothing to do what profits them alone. You have to act knowing that fact and make sure to overcome your enemies by what you decide to do."

"How can we fight the soldiers who are well-armed and take the citadel when we have no real weapons?" asked one man.

"You are right, Pedaros, we need weapons. For now, the sickles, axes, knives and clubs are enough, and with them the bows and arrows of the herders and the true aim of their arms with slings and stones. But it is our unity that is our most precious weapon. With unexpected surprise action, we will catch the garrison and landowners off-guard. Our first task is to take the citadel. There are fewer than sixty soldiers throughout the city and its surroundings. Its capture can be achieved if we devise a plan to approach and overcome the guards at the gate and seize their weapons, go to the prison to capture the soldiers and free those in chains, and then together all of us can overwhelm those in the square. Once we succeed in these actions, we will have more weapons and men to face the rest of the garrison at the camp. The city will be ours in little time. It will be easy after that to deal with the hired guards and other soldiers in the estates near Enna."

"And what happens after Enna?" inquired another herder Younis had met.

"Be assured, Dugga, that the rest of Sicilia will follow. Hundreds and thousands in cities and ports are ready to join us. I have heard reports of all those people unable to tolerate living in slavery's cage any longer. Others are waiting in places near and far, as you herders know well and have told each other and me. The gladiators will rise up and fight with us. Roma is busy with troubles at home and across the sea, in Attikís, in Iberia, Delos and other places. We will have a large army in a short time, and secure many cities and ports."

"Tell us what to do now, Younis."

"We cannot wait. We must act before suspicion is raised about our absence. Let us choose twelve men who will be the ones to approach the citadel gate." Nilos and Dugga stepped forward, and each of them called upon five men.

"Let us take an oath of faith in this action."

Younis picked up the studded cane and raised it. The men stood and moved toward him in a semicircle in front of the terrace.

"As men we swear to fulfill the will of the goddess."

"As men we swear to fulfill the will of the goddess."

"We will fight until all who breathe are free."

"We will fight until all who breathe are free."

"Let the earth quake by us, not only the gods this time. To freedom."

"To freedom," shouted the men in unison, and followed Younis and Nilos in the rush toward the citadel.

Chapter 15

It was late afternoon when the twelve men arrived at the gates of the citadel. They called out to the four soldiers standing on guard, who recognised them. As they approached the guards, they split into four groups, and each trio overpowered one of the guards. The soldiers were disarmed at knifepoint, offering little resistance as they were tied up. Nilos, Dugga and Manus each took up a shield and sword, handing the javelins and other shields, swords and daggers to others. Nilos raised the sword high and whistled a signal. The waiting crowd, armed with sickles, spades, clubs, axes and knives, and with Younis in the lead, rushed through the citadel gate and shut it behind them.

The prison was located not far from the gate at the southern fortifications, an eyesore to be kept out of sight. It could be approached without alerting residents or the garrison. A narrow alley with high stone walls on each side led to a small grassy mound that dipped toward the prison. This was not so much a building as a large deep cavern, fashioned out of the rocky hill with an entrance that has two barred, chained doors. Outside the prison, next to the massive doors lay a room used by soldiers. The three soldiers who emerged from the room were immediately surrounded. At the sight of so many in arms, they signalled immediate surrender by placing their right arms over their heads.

Younis and Nilos took the keys and unlocked the chains on the cavern entrance. Inside, light from the torches revealed a series of rooms formed by metal bars. Each cell held ten men, about forty in total. Younis and Nilos greeted the prisoners, most of them they knew well. The prisoners were confused to seeing fellow slaves, among them friends, take the place of soldiers. They seemed unsure whether to rejoice at this unexpected happening. Younis assured them they were being freed and told them to find their way carefully to the door and to assemble outside. Cheers erupted as the prisoners came out to the light and were embraced by friends. Younis called them all to attention and spoke:

"It is a moment of happiness to see you outside this horrible dungeon. I tell you that we have risked all to throw off this yoke forever. But we have no time to waste. Our liberty will only be temporary if we are not able to face the garrison and take the city. Those of you who are not able to fight can stay behind. We are many. Anyone willing to join us in the battle will make our victory only more certain."

All the prisoners, who knew the torment and inevitability of what otherwise had awaited them, expressed unhesitating desire to be part of the attack. Younis, scanning the prisoners, noticed that about fifteen of them looked particularly frail. He asked them to stay behind and trail them to inform others. It was just before dusk when the rebel throng moved into the city. Some citizens and landowners came out or peered from windows at the commotion, but most kept out of sight. Younis could not worry about any landowners or citizens at this moment and resolved to reach the square and then the garrison in time before sunset.

Other slaves joined them on the way, carrying any weapons they could find, as they immediately understood the nature of the fight and its implications for their lives. To add to the sickles, axes and other farming tools the rebels carried, the women quickly rushed out to distribute knives, clubs, more axes and other implements from kitchens and stores. Some who did not have shields had improvised by slitting open thick reed baskets or holding wide blocks of wood for protection.

The arms that these men carried would have been assessed as insufficient to secure a victory by soldiers and masters, but the resolve of those who desired to throw off the yoke of their oppression defied the conventions of the comfortable. It was the rightness of their cause that drove them now to believe in their own unity of purpose and place their faith in whatever natural forces or spirits would recognise their efforts as just. Most had never studied warfare or been trained to fight in a regular army. They readily adapted what they had learned of strategy in facing ever-changing circumstances, of survival skills in the struggle to stay alive without losing what remained of their dignity in forced bondage. These lessons imbued them with confidence to win this battle. It was an ineffable realization that at that moment neither a benevolent master nor any external force would regain their freedom. Only an inner transformation and their strength could overcome the challenge ahead.

Younis himself carried a shortsword and shield as he led the crowd, to the surprise of some. Not having been previously trained in warfare, Younis had sought out Nilos after their meeting. Perhaps in fortuitous anticipation, or perhaps simply as an expression of friendship, Nilos had dutifully taken him out to the woods alone over the past months. Using makeshift weapons, he trained him in basic defense, swordmanship and javelin throwing techniques. Younis even developed a particular expertise in hitting targets with small knives. Walking alongside him now, Nilos was anxious. He had privately ordered his trusted fighters to watch out for Younis, surround him when necessary, and to protect him at all costs.

As the square came into view, the first sight was that of the tops of the crucifixes, displaying the lifeless bodies that still hung from them. Five soldiers were just starting to lower the crucifixes as the rebel fighters charged into the square. The surprised soldiers dropped what they were carrying and drew their swords. Two were immediately struck unconscious and the other three surrounded and disarmed, and quickly restrained. The rebels now had five more shields, for a total of twelve, and an equal number of javelins, swords and daggers.

Younis decided to move on. There was no time to bring down the men from the crucifixes. He called Dugga, Manus and Nilos close to him.

"The coming battle will decide our fate. We need three squadrons of strong, well-armed men. Nilos, you take six shields and spears and head a group of fifty men in the front. Place the prisoners in front of you. Keep less armed men to the back, but ask them to press on when the fight starts. Once we engage the enemy, arch out with the shields into a half circle and push against the soldiers with the full force of all the men. Tell those who are carrying sickles and scythes to aim for the legs. Dugga and Manus, you take the remaining shields and spears and move behind with thirty men each. Manus, take the right, Dugga the left. When the battle begins, you two will circle out with your groups and attack the garrison formation from the flanks. Dugga, have fifteen archers ready should the garrison bring out their archers. If there are no archers, tell them to aim their arrows at the soldiers before you attack. Lead your men now and tell them what to do."

By the time the rebel fighters reached the camp, Spurius Dentatus, apparently forewarned by an informer, was already preparing to strike against them. Dentatus decided on a skirmishing formation. He had fewer than fifty soldiers standing in six rows of eight men. The lines were staggered and spaced some two paces apart. With shields upright and spears extended, they advanced until they reached about twenty paces from the crowd. Younis shouted for his men to stop and stepped forward.

"Centurio, we are more than three hundred and have your soldiers as prisoners in front of us. Even without arms we shall overcome you. You have a choice: fight and die, or surrender and lay down your arms. We have no intention to kill anyone. I promise not to harm you if you throw down your weapons." Younis called Dentatus *centurio* although he was not sure of his rank. Dentatus stepped out of the formation and delivered a challenge.

"You dare to speak to a commander of the empire so rudely, slave. We are soldiers of this realm and will destroy all who raise arms against it. If you stop now, you will be placed in chains but live. If you go on, you will be punished like the others who were crucified today."

"Your threat gives us grave concern. Let me talk to the men and see what they say." Younis went back behind the line and called Dugga, Manus and Nilos close to him: "Nilos, we attack the middle with the prisoners in front. Make sure to change your shields into a semi-circle upon attack. Once we engage, Dugga will circle out and attack from the side on the left. Manus, your men will attack from the right."

"Centurio Dentatus, since you desire a fight, we will oblige you."

Nilos shouted the order to attack. Soldiers started stabbing out with their spears as they moved ahead at those who got close, including their own men. Nilos reversed the direction of his front into a semi-circle, and pressed on with the crowd behind him. Soon the soldiers were unable to manoeuvre their spears or draw their swords. Now shields were pushing against shields, swords, daggers, axes, sickles and scythes slashing against flesh. The melee drove Nilos to fight on the right. Using his high reach, he pressed down with his shield and struck with his sword at the heads and necks over the shields, and then pushed the shields out to the side as he plowed through stabbing as he moved. Meanwhile, Dentatus was advancing in the centre, cutting into the crowd, and stabbed five men in succession. Dugga was enraged, but was not close enough to strike. Dugga and his men flanked the formation and with the spears brought down four enemy soldiers. Now Dugga sighted Dentatus close behind him. He sheathed his sword, shoving his way through with the shield. Taking out the club tied to his belt, he struck Dentatus on the side of his head. The helmet flew off. Without hesitating, Dugga again swung the club to hit the dazed Dentatus on his exposed skull. As they trampled on Dentatus, the soldiers were being gradually pushed back. Even as they continued to stab at the rebel fighters with their swords, one by one they were overwhelmed by three or four men pouncing on each of them from all sides. With their backs against a wall, seeing others downed and Dentatus brained, the remaining soldiers put their shields down, sheathed their swords and raised their right arms over their heads in surrender. Younis called on the men to stop.

It was well past dusk, darkness descending. More than thirty rebel fighters and twenty-five soldiers lay injured or dead, Dentatus among them. Nilos threw down the shield, walked up to Younis, and held his sword hand aloft. Raising his own bloodied sword high, he shouted: "Victory!"

Chapter 16

There would be no sleep until the whole city was secured. By late night the rebels were in control of Enna. The magistrate and his guards had been arrested, all placed in the chains and the prison they had used to incarcerate others. The landowners living in the city were taken and held in the two largest mansions, those of Damophilos and Secundus. Younis gave instructions that the landowners' children were to remain in their own houses under the protection of former slaves, who would now manage the properties.

Damophilos and other estates in the vicinity of Enna had to be dealt with next. Younis assembled his trusted companions, chief among them Dugga, who had distinguished himself in the attack on the garrison. Dugga was tasked with leading thirty well-armed men, including those who had been fighters and his fellow herders skilled in bow and arrow. The battalion was to proceed in five carriages to the Damophilos farm about three hours east of Enna. It was already well into the morning and the estate had to be reached before the trial ordered by Damophilos in mid afternoon. Dugga promised to get there sooner.

Orders were issued for collecting the bodies of the dead in the magistrate's house. Younis announced a burial ceremony to be held that afternoon for the crucified men, the women thrown off the cliff and those killed in the fighting. He ordered the arrest of any overseer or slave known to have had special allegiance to the landowners, anyone who had been willing to betray his fellows in bondage or to assist in inflicting cruelties. Roma and its followers would certainly be trying to plant spies and to buy traitors, both favourite methods they used to overcome rebellions and subdue cities. No one was to be left to roam who could prove harmful to the cause. Younis did not forget to send a man to the cave to bring Racilia. He gave a specific order to seize Juba, who did not take his arrest well, grovelling pitifully, screaming his allegiance and demanding to see Younis.

When Younis returned to the mansion, he found that Antigenes and Cassia had already been moved to the Damophilos estate with the other landowners. He did not have to face them right away, he thought, but Junia and Julian were still there and would have already seen what happened.

"Where are my parents?" asked Julian as both rushed toward him when they heard the commotion of his coming.

"Don't worry. No harm will come to them. They are with the others at the Damophilos mansion. You can go to see them there."

"They treated you well. How could you do this to them?" said Junia with obvious indignation.

Younis moved closer and placed one hand on Junia's shoulder, another on Julian's, who did not move. They must have surmised by then that Younis was in control, that he had the power to decide, and were balancing this unexpected turn against the long close relationship they had enjoyed with him for years. Younis sensed a rift already growing between them regardless. There was no remedy for this distance, even if he assured them their parents would not be mistreated.

"This has nothing to do with your parents. It could not be helped. All the events led to this necessity. All the cruelties and the killings forced us to act and end this oppression."

"What's going to happen to them?"

"The assembly will meet and decide. I am certain those who committed no atrocity will be released to go back to the peninsula, no need to be concerned," Younis reassured them again. "Do not worry," he said as they seemed to calm down. "This mansion will be busy with activity. It is better for you to stay with your friend Perpetua until matters are resolved in a few days."

Attending to Perpetua was more difficult. Megalis was among those arrested and put in prison, as would Damophilos when brought in. Both their fates seemed to be sealed. Younis sent a message to Lamia to bring Perpetua to him. He had given explicit instructions to those who were making arrests not to mistreat or abuse anyone, and that any punishment to be handed down to previous masters or mistresses would be decided in public trial by the assembly. In the case of Perpetua, it was unlikely that anyone would think of causing her harm or insult anyway since all knew her to be different and remembered her compassion and her attempts to shield those in her household from punishment. While Younis intended to try to make her understand, he knew that ultimately there was no way to mitigate her suffering at what might happen to her parents. How could he save her and perhaps himself from fearing the worst? How could she possibly accept or forgive?

When she came in with Lamia her face was a veil that he could not guess what lay behind. It surprised Younis how much she had matured in the months since he last saw her, and she was still wearing the amulet.

"Perpetua, you are dear to us," he started. "You can see that everything has changed. There will be more that will happen. It is better that we send you away to a safer place."

She did not answer right away. Her first utterance was not unexpected, but it still startled Younis.

"Where's my mother?"

He decided to tell her what was only enough. "In this situation, we must take precautions. We cannot leave those who can harm us to act or to send messages. Your mother is being held away from the angry crowds, and your father will be here later in the day. They will be judged by the assembly along with all the others to decide their fate. We will arrange for you to go to Missina with those who are released, and from there to your relatives in the peninsula. In the meantime, Junia and Julian will be staying with you."

Perpetua was silent for a while and looked at him uncertainly. She was obviously confused about all the changes and the unknown ahead, and was probably beginning to understand it was futile to ask for her mother and father to accompany her. Then she uttered her second question, which was more difficult for Younis to handle.

"Will my parents be killed?"

"I cannot be sure what the assembly will decide," he answered, aware of being evasive. "It is unusual what has happened. Do not blame us for what we did and what we will do, which has to be done. You find it hard to appreciate this now. Maybe you will later. My hope is for a better tomorrow and for you all future happiness," he said knowing full well that happiness would be hard to find soon, and that the outcome for her parents was inevitable, and impossible for her to accept.

Would she implore him to influence the assembly to show mercy? Would she want to wait to see the verdict on her parents being carried out? Instead, she asked if she could see them before leaving, and said in a tone that could have been both suppliant and reproachful, "I wish you and the people well." As Lamia was escorting her out, Perpetua turned toward Younis as if to tell him something she could not say, and then moved her hand in a small wave of farewell. He raised his hand too, realising that they would never see each other again.

Younis decided that should the assembly condemn Damophilos, Megalis and Cornelia, all three would be thrown off the cliff. There would be no tortures or crucifixions. The executions would be delayed until after Perpetua's departure.

Chapter 17

Dugga and his fighters outdid expectations. When they arrived back in Enna in the late afternoon, the carriages they took and additional carriages they brought with them were loaded with scores of men and women and children from the estate and surrounding area. They had apprehended Damophilos during his repast, along with his guards and eunuchs. Dugga told Younis that several other people who could not come in the carriages were walking toward Enna and would arrive by nightfall. Younis expressed concern about this movement, perhaps the people wanted to celebrate, and told Dugga that they would have to be persuaded to return to manage the estates and continue the farming and other essential work there. Among those who joined the carriages on horseback, Dugga reported, was a horse trainer called Akhaeus from the Cinna estate. That reminded Younis that he had seen Akhaeus some months before and spoke to him. Akhaeus, who carried the name of a mythical hero and the region of his birth Akhaia, was a young fighter in Korinthos during its destruction, and will certainly be an asset to have in the war council.

Three days after the victory, Younis decided to hold a public trial of landowners to determine what to do with them. He realised that victory had brought a sense of fulfillment for the fighters, but they also needed some measure of justice, especially over the dreadful loud predictions threatened by the more stubborn among the captured landowners. This trial would not be an act of vengeance, a repetition of the blood and torture they had suffered at the hands of slaveholders, but the first step in redemption through the freedom they had earned. He ordered callers with drums to announce an assembly of all the people in the amphitheatre at noon on the following day.

The theatre was crowded with liberated slaves and several of Enna's Sicilian citizens. As the landowners were ushered in or, when necessary, dragged into the centre of the amphitheatre, they were met with heckles, shouts and curses, most of them directed at Damophilos, Megalis, Cornelia, and a few others. The landowners displayed various reactions, from utter disorientation to haughty pride, their faces looking generally befuddled at this turn of events. A few may have felt less guilty about their treatment of slaves, and so were more dignified in posture and resigned to the outcome. But overall, a puzzled air pervaded among the landowners, as did the hapless belief that this situation was a momentary humiliation. The Sicilian citizens were somewhat subdued, as it seemed they had come to watch rather than to participate. Most of them were not well off, and only a few could afford to own a slave. They were anxious about how to take this reversal, especially in view of recent memory of the vengeance meted out against the citizens of any city for switching allegiance or wanting to have their own rule.

Loud cheers erupted as Younis appeared on the balcony with Elissar and behind them Nilos, Hermon, Dugga and others.

"Younis, Younis, Younis."

He waited until the crowd quieted down.

"We are here and we are free." The crowd rose up again in shouts and chants.

"Today we celebrate our self-rule in Enna. To make it secure for the future, we cannot wait long to spread our fight against injustice to the whole island and beyond, to break the bonds of all who have been enslaved against their will, to institute new laws that treat all human beings with equality. You can be certain Roma will be sending its armies against us. We must be prepared to face them, and we will be. Right now, there is one grave task that is required of us. It falls to you to judge those who have oppressed you, to decide the fate of these landowners who enriched themselves at your expense and did the bidding of their masters in Roma. On them must be applied the common laws of human justice. These laws we understand. They are not the laws and dictates of Roma, which serve the few and instill in them the belief that they are better than others. The true laws we know are those inherited from the gods and goddesses and are given to all beings. Their precepts are evident. They tell us to honour human life and respect the natural world that sustains us. Their decrees ask us to be merciful. They also command us to be firm, to level punishment against those who do harm to the body and spirit of the human family. Let us then agree to judge these landowners and their wives by the most sacred decrees and laws. Let those who are good be respected, and let those who are evil be punished, even struck down. Those who care for others should be honoured whereas those who abuse others should be shunned. Those who save the lives of others should have their just reward whereas those who torture and kill without cause should suffer the same fate as their victims."

The crowd replied with shouts and cheers of acclamation.

"We will in due time issue edicts and set up courts and appoint judges to deal with matters of daily life. Now about these landowners, we need to have your voices to decide. I will name them one by one, each of them and their wives. Those among you who are witnesses should come forward and tell us what they know. The landowners and their wives are allowed to answer any accusations."

Damophilos walked forward and interjected: "You and the others should know we are citizens of Roma and so must be judged by the laws of Roma. As you know this rebellion is … ." A loud clamour from the crowd drowned out his voice.

"Let him speak. Let us see what comes out of his mouth," said Younis. "You will be judged for what you did by the laws of the world, as Younis said," answered Hermias, formerly a slave in one of Damophilos' estates.

Damophilos then turned in the direction of a section of Sicilian citizens, and addressed them: "This rebellion has been won for today in Enna. But it is doomed to fail in the end. Roma will be sending its legions to destroy it. You do not want to be on the losing side of this battle that will surely come. If we are harmed, your fate is certain. It is better to release us to go to Roma and plead with the senate to show mercy and even make reforms that will improve your condition. The situation will be restored to its normal state and your lives will be saved." Unable to come to terms with the loss of his power, Damophilos ended in a flourish, convinced that he had made a winning argument.

Hermias started to take out his sword while Damophilos was speaking but sheathed it again and replied: "Your plea is a trick to save yourself. You have long treated everyone else with contempt and cruelty, considering us all gullible and worthless. You cannot gain our support or pity now. Your promises are intended to deceive us and will be forgotten if we agree to them. You and Roma no longer hold power over us. We know Roma's mercy from what happened in the past and what is still happening in other places. We do not trust you or the senate or the legions of Roma."

An old Sicilian, Duketios, stood up and asked to be allowed to speak. The crowd went silent and listened carefully to his words.

"As a humble citizen of this city, I want to say that we do not take sides in this quarrel. I remember much of what happened when I was young, or heard it from my father and grandfather. Now that I am old, I see that this turn of events is not totally unexpected. Much needed to be improved in how the city and this island were ruled. Justice was seldom respected, and abuses were many. Roma should have seen the wisdom of preventing these acts of cruelty, which could have saved us from this unrest and its dire consequences."

"You have spoken well, Duketios. We understand that you have to speak with caution. What we have done was necessary to do and cannot be undone. Now we have to decide the fate of these landowners who were sent here by Roma to exploit this island."

Zeuxis stood up: "I used to be a slave of this man Damophilos, whom I hesitate to call human. He is evil incarnate. Beyond his constant insults, he delighted in having me punished in cruel ways for trivial and dubious reasons, as he did with many others. He ordered countless executions—some for those who attempted to escape and others for offenses that did not warrant the taking of life. He made himself judge and executioner, and enjoyed killing. His wife Megalis did the same, at times even surpassing her husband in the perverse happiness she derived from the suffering of others. They are both responsible for torturing and murdering many of our friends and relatives. If we are to apply the laws Younis mentioned, or by any other human law, they must be punished for their crimes in the same way that they took other lives." Others spoke to verify these accusations and gave personal accounts of what had happened to them and their friends.

Younis called out the names of Damophilos and Megalis again, and asked people to declare their verdict of condemnation by raising their hands. The liberated slaves stood up en masse, raising their arms high. Megalis went into a fit of crying, and collapsed to the ground. Damophilos, who looked stern but walked unsteadily, helped her to stand up. Cornelia's name was called next. She received the same sentence, on the evidence from those in her mansion that she had approved of the four men to be crucified and had personally chosen the two women to be thrown off the cliff.

With the other landowners Gaius Petronius, Calestrius Tiro, Fulvius Trimalcio, and Gaius Dasumius, several witnesses came forward to report occasional minor punishment and withholding of food and supplies. Younis proposed that they be kept in custody until further consideration, which received the assembly's consent. Next were Pedanius Antigenes, Claudius Etruscus, Calpurnius Fabatus, Toranius Flaccus, Longinus Castor, Claudius Acusilaus, and Cornelius Cinna, and their wives and children. Witnesses agreed that their treatment was usually equitable, that they provided adequate supplies for the sustenance of those who served them, that they were not inclined to cruelty, and that while some of their overseers committed abuses, they themselves did not participate. Younis suggested that these people should be released and pledged their safe passage to the peninsula. This was not simply a gesture of goodwill, but also a demonstration of their true aim—to throw off the shackles of bondage rather than to exact revenge. Separating the landowners in this way showed justness and equity. The people realised instinctively that an otherwise undifferentiated judgement would have undermined the nobleness of their cause and its future.

As the landowners were escorted out, Etruscus turned toward Younis and said aloud: "You have kept your word for sure, to become king. I did not believe it then and did not think it would happen. We do not agree with you, but what you did today shows that you are indeed a man of honour who deserves respect."

Antigenes and Cassia walked toward Younis. It was an awkward moment. Younis sensed that both of them needed to say words, and he wanted to assure them that none of this had anything to do with his feelings toward them. Antigenes looked solemn and clearly displeased, but he managed to say in a quiet and plain voice:

"I have talked with Cassia about this. We do not understand your actions and find them to be unjustified. We gave you no cause for what you did. We are losing our home and our lands. We can only say to you that we hope to get them back soon. But we still appreciate what you did to teach the children and what you did today not to let revenge be vented blindly."

"Be sure that I also appreciate your good treatment of me as your slave," Younis said. "Let us not quibble now about who owns the land. You know as much as I that what happened is bigger than you or me. It could not be helped. Events reached a head and could not be stopped."

"We cannot predict what will happen next," Antigenes said, perhaps suggesting that Hypsaeus and Roma's legions would be coming.

"We plan to make a new beginning, to succeed in what we have started, but we will surely fight any force sent to stop us," Younis anticipated.

Antigenes started moving away, but Cassia stayed and said to Younis:

"We wish no harm to come to you."

"I spoke with Junia and Julian and assured them of your safety. Perpetua will be going with you to be delivered to her relatives near Roma. She is a young woman now, but she will need your help to overcome what will happen to her parents. I wish you well in your travels and hope for your happiness in the future."

"We shall inquire about Perpetua's relatives. If there is any difficulty in finding them, we will treat Perpetua as our own child," added Cassia, walking toward Antigenes.

The next morning, those to be released were escorted to their own mansions to prepare for departure. Each family was given one of its own carriages, and five mounted fighters were to escort the convoy halfway to Katane.

Chapter 18

Younis assembled a council of war comprised of those who distinguished themselves in combat: Dugga, Nilos, Manus, Hermon, and Munim. He also sought out Akhaeus the horse trainer, and Yousif, a spirited young man from ʿAkka with unusual reddish hair who had performed remarkable feats of bravery. To their number, he added two metalsmiths, Bion and Athalos, as well as the carpenter Fuabal, each one a skilled practitioner of their respective crafts. Younis chose the dining hall in the Antigenes mansion as a command centre. The men had not seen this hall, and some had never even been inside a mansion. Unused to such luxury they stared in amazement at the large painted panels and various artifacts. On the main table, Younis made sure to place only two simple amphorae of water and wine and two bowls of grapes and figs.

"We are meeting here to seek advice and help from each other. I chose this place where I used to perform for the landowners to tell you that we have earned the right to occupy and use it, though we will not partake of the luxurious habits of its past owners, if indeed they could rightly claim ownership. You have shown bravery in the battle and taken the risks that brought us to meet on this momentous day. You led your men and inspired them to feats of courage to achieve this great victory that many thought impossible. Your actions inspired awe in our foes and loyalty among our people."

"It is your wise leadership and shrewd plans that made what happened possible," Dugga responded, mirroring the sentiment of others around the table.

"You are the one who finished Dentatus so adeptly. Nilos stood so tall in the fight, and those with him, and you Manus, Hermon, Munim, Yousif and the others, all pushed the rest of the garrison to its surrender. You did much more than implement a plan."

Younis continued: "But this is only the beginning, as you know. The future will bring unforeseen challenges that require resilience and fortitude. We must prepare and be ready. Since Hypsaeus will be moving against us soon, our greatest urgency is to make sure that we are equipped for war. Above all, we need to train more fighters and find weapons for them. To stay in Enna and wait would be dangerous. It may be what Roma expects us to do, to stay and defend the city. That seems at first to be the easiest course. It will not last, and it well could be our downfall. The whole island is our best defense. We must work to get more men and women and other cities to join us, and continue to strengthen our forces so we can stand against the legions in the field of battle."

"How much time do we have before Hypsaeus attacks?" asked Nilos, who was sitting next to Younis.

Akhaeus signaled that he wanted to speak. "Even when he gets the news in Katane in a few days, it will not be possible for him to move right away. He does not have sufficient force and will have to wait for enforcements from other cities and instructions from the senate. If he asks for troops from Roma, it will take several weeks to get an answer and still more time for them to arrive. Winter is coming, so he may decide to delay attack until early spring. It could come in a month at the earliest, but most likely it will be in three or four."

Younis still expressed reservations: "Roma may consider it too dangerous to leave our success unchallenged which could serve as fuel for other dissatisfactions, and so order him to move sooner. We must be alert, post sentries in all directions, and send out small parties farther afield. He will approach from the east. Our shepherd friends should be informed to ask other shepherds for what they see and hear. When Hypsaeus does move, we must confront him before he gets to Enna, and in a place of our choosing."

"I will arrange for this communication immediately with my men, and tell others we trust who are in the fields. We will have eyes and ears even in Katane itself."

"That is good, Dugga. Many have joined already. We have more than five thousand men and a good number of women in Enna alone. We expect many from other far-flung estates and mansions, and thousands from neighbouring cities. The farmers and shepherds have started to come over to our side in greater numbers. But weapons and training are what we need. What was taken from the soldiers until now, from the guards and the mansions, equips only a few hundreds. We must get more swords, shields, daggers, javelins, pikes, armour, bows and arrows, slings, as well as ballistas, catapults, siege towers, and much more. Tell me, Athalos and Bion, what can you and other blacksmiths produce in swords, javelins and arrows in one month's time?"

"There are five blacksmiths in the city," Athalos responded, holding a fig. "Not all are weapon-makers. If we get help from carpenters and others, we may be able to make five or six hundred swords, perhaps not all of the best quality, a similar number of shields, and about two thousand points for javelins and arrows."

"We must have more than that. You have authority to recruit other craftspeople, as many as possible, and anyone else whose skills can be used, including Enna citizens. Tell us if anyone refuses to help. We cannot allow any waning in this effort. The skills of our women should not be forgotten in recruiting helpers."

"Bion and I will immediately set up a group to do this work with speed."

"Those who were fighters before shall train others to be fighters, and this is to begin right away, even before more weapons are made."

Nilos was eager to speak. "As one who was a gladiator, I suggest it would be very useful to bring in as many gladiators as possible from other cities. They will be most dependable in training others for battle both here in Enna and where they are now. We only need to free them and they will immediately join the fight. Katane we cannot enter yet. The closest other city with a gladiator camp is

Siracusai." Nilos held a small cluster of grapes. "The product of my labour," he whispered to himself, and continued. "Even if the entire garrison is still there, a small force can enter secretly, release the gladiators, and with them overcome the soldiers and liberate the city. Siracusai will add to our strength."

"That's a great plan. It should be executed at once. Go ahead, Nilos. Quickly choose as many men as you need, a hundred or more, and march on Siracusai tomorrow."

"Once Siracusai is freed you can decide who is to be left in charge of the city and how many gladiators to bring here," Younis added. "Our aim is to have an army that is different from the legions. No doubt, we will need an infantry with swords, shields and javelins, but we cannot hope to train enough people until later. Let us marshal our immediate advantage. Right now, our best asset lies in the skills of our herders and shepherds who already master the sling, the club, and the bow and arrow. They can form our most moveable force once they are marshalled into organised units."

"There is a good number of them already," Dugga replied. "I will call in more from those in the field and put together troops of archers trained for action."

"And I will find the ones who are skilled with slings," Munim added with enthusiasm. "They will be a surprise to our enemies for sure. Many are so sharp they can hit a small animal with a stone from 300 paces."

"What worries me most is the cavalry. We must find ways to oppose it," Younis said. Others also expressed anxiety about facing the legions without a cavalry. Akhaeus suggested they start by preparing pikes to be used by the first lines of infantry, though that strategy works only for the first direct attack and would be insufficient alone to deal with the quicker movement by enemy cavalry on the field. In terms of supply of horses, Akhaeus added, there was little difficulty in bringing hundreds from the horse farms.

"The best solution is to have a strong cavalry of our own. But starting an effective cavalry requires a lot of training. I heard of the right person to command a cavalry if we can somehow convince him to join our side," Yousif said.

"Who is he?" The question came from Manus and almost at the same time from others.

"His name is Kleon, an overseer from Taormina. He has broken out of the law with his brother Komanos. The garrisons have sent scouts to scour the countryside in search of his hideout. It is said he does marvels with horses, and is already in the forests with many men."

"Let us try to find him then."

"We have scouts who can be trusted to search for him. Akhaeus and I, and Yousif with us, may be able to help in tracking him," Munim proposed. "We will go out and inquire from shepherds in the mountains west of Taormina."

"By all means, take a group and proceed as quickly as possible. It will be a boon to have someone like him with us."

Younis turned to Nilos: "Nilos, as you embark on your mission, our hearts are with you," and then addressed the others: "What we have planned today gives me great assurance that we will succeed. Let us now do what we have agreed. I bid you all farewell until we meet again."

The men stayed behind briefly to talk and exchange thoughts. As they parted, they clasped arms and embraced. All shared in a sense of cheer and hope.

Chapter 19

Seven days later, Kleon and his followers rode into Enna. Munim, Akhaeus and Yousif rode at his side, as did his brother Komanos with them. Kleon had been located in the forests of the Nebrodi Mountains near Traina. It was not easy to find him since he used to change camp every two or three days. As he moved from camp to camp more men followed him, so the number had grown to more than three hundred mounted fighters.

Kleon's long blonde hair flew back in the strong wind, along with it the trailing mane of his white horse. His body was fully armoured right down to the greaves on his legs, a feathered helmet tied to the back of his saddle and his round leopard-embossed shield slung on the other side. The sight amazed those lined up in welcome on the road leading up to the citadel. They cheered the convoy, many sounding tambourines and drums, while others handed bouquets of flowers to the riders or sprinkled petals in their path. The rumbling of so many hoofs reverberating across the hills brought excitement and joy to the people, reassuring them. Here was the beginning of a great army that would grow and help to defend them.

Dugga and his men were waiting just inside the city gate. Munim dismounted and went up to meet Dugga. He then returned to Kleon and asked him to tell his men to stay behind with Dugga, who would take them to a banquet hall for food and later to their lodging in various mansions.

Munim and Akhaeus escorted Kleon to the Antigenes mansion. As Kleon dismounted, Younis walked up to him, smiling, and extended his arm in greeting. The two figures stood in extreme contrast: Younis in a simple tunic, dark hair and beard, Kleon fully armoured, a bit taller with blonde hair and red-tinged beard. Younis pulled Kleon closer, so their shoulders touched.

"We are most happy you are with us."

"I am pleased to be here, and to see what you have begun and done already."

The dining room table was set up for a meal, but there were no attendants. Younis poured a drink for Kleon and for himself, and expecting that Kleon would want food after the journey did not ask questions right away. As Kleon was eating, Younis took the time to tell him about events that transpired in Enna, what led to the resolve to start the uprising, how the city was taken, and what the assembly decided about the landowners.

"I commend your decision to release some of them, but I doubt it will bring about any change in how Roma will behave and what it will do."

"We did not do it for the sake of getting any good treatment from the rulers in Roma. We did it to establish equity and justice that will rule all of us as free people. It is best that people have some hope to look for in the future, to live by laws that are fair and just. We did not envisage that anything good would be gained by replacing cruel bondage with unruly chaos."

"That is wise. It is how I felt about my men and their future when we were in the woods. I could not see the end of a journey if we remained on the run, with all our energies sapped as we try to defend ourselves and escape all the time."

"Tell me how you came to be in the woods."

"As you know, I come from Kilikia near Tarsos."

"Tarsos, it's not too far from where I was born in Afamia, some days up the coast by carriage, or by boat," Younis interrupted.

"I have heard of Afamia. My brother Komanos and I were recruited into the war that was coming our way from the west when we were barely old enough to fight. We came from a tribe that bred and herded horses. From childhood we were adept at training animals for racing and use by the cavalry."

"Yes, horses are the companions of warriors. They bring blessings and good fortune."

"Both of us were captured in a battle with Roma's legions in Hellas."

"These wars were going on long before too. My father fought and was killed in those same wars."

"It must have been hard for your mother and for you. Indeed, it was a difficult time for all our people. Luckily, maybe because of our skill with horses, my brother and I were kept together and shipped to Sicilia to work on a large horse farm near Taormina. We were unhappy, but we kept our feelings to ourselves, always thinking and talking about what to do to escape. The same army that enslaved us we were helping by supplying its cavalry with trained horses. We decided to bide our time, and coached other slaves in the estate. It was easy to convince the landlord, who was happy to see his farm prosper and sell more horses to the legions. It took more than four years for the opportune moment to arrive. With a trusted group we overcame the guards, took all the horses and weapons we could find, and lit out into the woods. As we moved from place to place, we collected more weapons and men, even women who were willing to join us."

"It would be most favourable for us to fight together."

"For me, it will fulfill a dream I have had of fighting in a great army to bring about a better life for the people. I am sure my men will agree. But I must speak to them and give each one a choice whether to remain here or return to the woods."

"Know, my friend, we plan to collect all the horses from the estates around us and other places we gain on the island. There is no worry about numbers. Many men and even women, I heard, are eagerly waiting to join your cavalry."

Younis explained to Kleon more about what had been achieved in preparations. A confluence of factors was helping to bolster their cause, an opportunity for alliances among various groups. Though many Sicilian citizens remained cautious, anxious at the memory of past retaliation, a great number of farmers and herdsmen were already joining, having lived so long in fear and everyday inequity, they yearned to be rid of the bonds that forced them to expend their strength in labours while profits accrued to landowners appointed by Roma. The slaves freed by this rebelllion came from various regions far and wide across the sea and beyond. It was a singular historic moment for humans to break the chains of bondage and to end injustice. These were not only physical chains, but also even more pernicious chains—chains that pressed them into resignation to another's will over their lives and encased their minds in fear and degradation. Many more thousands would surely rise with them, and with his help a great army can be marshaled to defeat the legions.

An attendant knocked on the door and told Younis a messenger had just galloped into the city with an urgent report. Younis went out, soon came back and walked toward Kleon with excitement:

"You are the first to hear of this. We have just received great news. Our friend Nilos has liberated the gladiators in Siracusai. The city is ours. Tomorrow or the day after you will meet him and the gladiators he brings. He will tell us of his feats."

Chapter 20

In the evening before the final march to face Hypsaeus, Younis called all the fighters to congregate in the valley where they had camped. He had walked around camp earlier in the day and spoke to smaller groups, but he wanted all the fighters to hear his words together before this battle. Nilos, Kleon, Dugga. Akhaeus, Munim and other commanders stood beside him on a mound, wearing assorted helmets and armour. Younis was ready too, not wanting his people to think he would let them go to battle alone. He had followed up on earlier training by Nilos and further enhanced his fighting skills over the past few months. He donned a simple Illyrian-type bronze helmet, with a large opening for the face, that Bion had crafted with silver gilding and two lions carved on each side. His body was covered in light chainmail armour to the knees, with a finely embossed cuirass on top. On his side he carried a shortsword, and to his saddle were tied an axe and a pouch containing very small knives.

The animated crowd grew silent when Younis raised his arm. Holding high his studded chestnut cane he commenced to speak:

"Men and women, this battle we are about to fight is indeed greater and more momentous than anyone could imagine. To the surprise of your oppressers, you have thrown off the heavy yoke that was pressed around your necks. You used to serve those who thought of themselves as masters above you, entitled to own you as property. You herded sheep and cattle and farmed the land wholly for their benefit and profit. Some of you served in their mansions, cooked their food, bathed them, cared for their children, and provided them with every luxury. The brutality of empire had conspired to defeat your countries and turn you into people to be exploited, without any rights. Those landowners congratulated themselves, much pleased to get free labour after placing you in chains of servility. You tolerated their insults and their abuses, thinking at times that they were strong and you were weak. You are not weak anymore. You are stronger than your enemies, and you are now free!"

The crowd erupted in cheers as Younis uttered these words, raising their weapons high in the air.

"You no longer work for those self-appointed lords, the greedy men into whose hands the empire had placed you. You now know that they always feared you and what you could achieve once you gathered together and rose up against their brutality. Together you are strong, and your cause is most just. You are here united in the risks of bravery to fight for freedom in greater numbers than ever before assembled. Your uprising has already succeeded in what has never before been achieved on this island, or anywhere else. Encouraged by your brave actions, people in bondage are rising against tyranny in many places far and near, even in Roma itself.

"The lords of Roma are sending their legions against us. They want to take you back in time, to place the yoke around your necks again and to end your hopes for a new life. They think they can make you an example for others who have been downtrodden to prevent them from raising their heads. They want to continue buying and selling you for coins, as they do with bags of grain or herds of cattle, and to abuse your bodies and your souls to benefit their lives of profit and ease.

"This is the moment that will determine whether we make permanent what we have achieved with our own hands and make sure that we will never be dispossessed again, never again be forced to accept servitude. Only a few days ago, you showed your great spirit as you turned those who oppressed you into helpless fools and handed them the fate they deserve. You punished those who deserved retribution, and the others we loaded onto carriages and sent back to their arrogant masters in Roma.

"If tomorrow you show the same spirit, victory will be ours. All around us are the hills, plains and forests of this island, beyond them the seas that encircle it. There is no place else to go. As you meet your enemies you must be victorious. Only by winning the battle will there be honour and eternal life in the memory of all humanity.

"Do not imagine that victory will be difficult as the fame of war may suggest. If you put up a great fight, no power can defeat you. Some may think we are facing the army of an empire. The men we will be fighting have no great purpose. They fight for the promise of booty if they survive. For too long, those emboldened by their weaponry have devised their trickeries and believe that their false gods approve. Because they have suffered only small opposition, they feel entitled to continue to profit from their cruel abuses. Their armies protect themselves with helmets and shields, and will use brute force if they think they are winning. But they will run away when they see they are losing and are about to die.

"Remember this: if we fall into their hands in defeat, we will receive the cruelest of tortures, the ugliest and most ignominious of deaths. We cannot be timid or hesitant.

"We exceed them not only in numbers, but in will and purpose. We have nothing more to fear, for we have already lived many years in fear of punishment and death. We aspire for liberty and fight for dignity. We have a higher hope and a greater spirit. Our hearts are on fire with indignation, spurred by determination never to return to past humiliation. You are new-born with endless courage and eternal aim. Your gods are the gods of justice. You must therefore set aside as absolutely impossible any result other than to overcome the enemy. If you are firmly resolved on this and it is fixed in your minds, I say again you have already won the battle. Believe that to be happy means to be free and to be free means to be courageous.

"We will not go lightly into the perils of this war. We have already made our choices and decided on a plan to defeat this enemy. We have prepared a surprise for Hypsaeus and his army from which they will not recover. Our cavalry, infantry and archers will appear when least expected and will surely wreak havoc on Roma's legions. In the morning, we march to our chosen locations. We will be ready to show them our mettle in battle. Rest well tonight. Tomorrow is the day you will remember for the rest of your lives. It is a day that will live on in the memory of all generations to come."

Chapter 21

"They are across the bridge, about eight thousand, lightly armed, and less than two hundred on horseback," reported the lead explorator to Lucius Plauci Hypsaeus.

"It will be an easy rout."

Hypsaeus had received news of the revolt while in Katane, and immediately sent a message to the senate describing the situation as best he could, despite contradictory reports, giving an estimate of the rebel force. He informed the senate that he could not put together more than one legion and a half, and that he needed at least three legions for the action to subdue Enna. Within two weeks he was told that the senate would be sending one more legion, and instructed him to recruit more Sicilians to reinforce his numbers and to call in soldiers from garrisons in nearby cities. The senators had concluded based on past experience that the slave rebellion was limited to Enna and could be handled by Hypsaeus without more reinforcement. For them, this foolish uprising by the weak with untutored leaders at their head must be summarily extinguished, and they expected Hypsaeus to accomplish the task with speed. In reality, the reason the senate could not send more legions had to do with pressing matters elsewhere, in particular the need to deploy forces in the peninsula to counter other unrest, especially in Etruria, and to deal with other rebellions. Most worrying was the situation in Iberia, where the shepherd Viriato continued to harass the legions in an unconventional war of ambushes and raids. Even in Roma itself, several hundred slaves had risen up upon hearing of events in Enna.

It was early spring by the time Hypsaeus was ready to move from Katane. While waiting for reinforcements, he thought it best to delay to avoid the winter weather. He proceeded toward Enna with more than three legions. On the third night, he set up camp near Nissuria, just west of Agira. On the fourth day, after ordering the troops to break camp with the intention of marching to Enna, he received a surprise report of rebel forces on the other side of the Asura Bridge. Being informed by shepherds of legion movements, Younis had decided on this spot to meet Hypsaeus before he could reach Enna. By this time, the rebel army numbered in excess of thirty thousand, most of them already well-trained fighters, along with Kleon's cavalry which had more than doubled to a thousand strong.

The long Asura Bridge did not cross a river but overpassed a deep ravine extending northwest to southeast. Younis and his war council had decided to outwit the enemy by keeping only about a third of their forces visible, while Kleon's cavalry, some infantry, the larger part of Dugga's archers and Munim's slingers were to stay hidden from view until the start of battle. Most of the hills were low-lying, known intimately by the shepherds who traversed these lands during various seasons. Just northwest of the bridge a particularly high hill, heavily treed, descended sharply to the edge of the road a few hundred paces from the north entrance to the bridge. It was on this hill that Dugga lay hidden with most of the bowmen and Munim with the slingers, and beyond a cluster of trees just north Kleon's cavalry were ready to go into action at the appointed time. Some rebel infantry, armed with swords, shields, axes, sickles, spades, clubs and javelins, was kept in reserve to join Dugga, Munim and Kleon in their surprise attack on the legion's rear.

When Hypsaeus crossed the bridge, he could see rebel infantry about eight hundred paces ahead. More than two-thirds of his army had not crossed yet or were still crowded on the bridge when Younis ordered the attack. His aim was to hold Hypsaeus in check as long as possible and prevent those bottled up on the bridge from crossing. Seeing the rebels moving toward him, Hypaseus had no choice but to order a counterattack by the infantry that had crossed and a small part of his cavalry. The cavalry was less than a hundred paces away when the front rebel line gave way and out came about thirty men, three deep across the road, carrying long pikes. Hemmed in by dense shrubs and rocks on both sides, the first line of cavalry was in gallop and had no way of avoiding the points of the pikes against either themselves or their horses. In almost no time the road was littered with dead or injured men and horses, which completely hampered the advance of those behind them.

At this point, the signal went up for Dugga, Munim and Kleon to attack the columns backed up north of the bridge. Dugga unleashed a barrage of arrows onto the flank of Hypsaeus' infantry and cavalry. They were caught by surprise and unable at first to use their shields for protection. Munim and his slingers then moved closer and unloaded their javelins against the horses and their riders, before using their slings to target the infantry. The well-timed showers of arrows forced Hypsaeus' infantry to adjust its formation to face the unexpected side attack. In the thick of battle, Dugga and a small squadron rushed ahead into enemy lines forced to back up against the bridge. It was a move that almost cost Dugga his life. He was slashed in the side and fell, but was immediately rescued by his men. And this squadron was being surrounded and would have been overwhelmed and finished off were it not that Kleon and his men rumbled in, along with the reserve rebel infantry. That's when the enemy infantry and cavalry retreated toward the east in disarray.

Hypsaeus did not expect what happened in front of him, or at his back. His surprise grew as rebel movements and numbers multiplied. He was beginning to hear alarms on the north side of the bridge and distant cries of panic. When his prefect reported what was happening behind them at the bridge, Hypsaeus decided to go back. He calculated that he could hold the north end of the bridge easily, and at the same time launch a counterattack. This action was too late, and movement back proved difficult at every step. When he arrived to the other end of the bridge, he found a large part of his army already cut down by slings and arrows, dead or injured, or fleeing the assault by Kleon. Hypsaeus advanced in support of those still standing their ground in some spots, but he realised right away that it was a hopeless fight. The rebels were too many and could not be driven back. Some of his remaining cavalry was by then on foot and others were chasing after horses to attempt an escape. Kleon had space to manoeuvre and was hacking at the backs of the retreating lines, with the rebel infantry and slingers advancing in support behind him.

As he was trying to rally his forces, Hypsaeus was shocked by a sling that scraped his arm and unhorsed him. Immediately scrambling back on his mount, he surveyed the battlefield, and concluding the battle was lost he ordered the trumpets to sound retreat. He did not stay long in his camp two miles to the east. After waiting the rest of the day for any fleeing infantry to arrive, he determined it was best to return to Katane early the next morning.

The women's ululations rang across the hills in celebration of the victory. Other than those who had joined Kleon's cavalry, more than a hundred women had escorted the rebel force and were gathered behind the battle lines. They crossed the bridge with Younis and immediately, along with men who also knew the arts of wound-healing, started tending to the injured. Younis gave instructions to his escorts to make sure to secure the enemy injured in one location and to order prisoners to dig burial pits.

With Hypsaeus in retreat, Younis decided further action would be opportune. He called a meeting of his commanders. Some thought there was no time to waste, that they should immediately pursue Hypsaeus to his camp and destroy what remained of his army. Younis suggested instead that since Hypsaeus had lost half his army and would be slowed down by remnants of his infantry the time was ripe to liberate Katane and Taormina, thus gaining wider support for the rebellion. Kleon's cavalry could outmanoeuvre Hypsaeus by getting to the east coast first to capture Katane before he reached it. This would accomplish the same purpose by forcing Hypsaeus to retreat further north, and bring more people into the revolt. Kleon proposed to take most of his cavalry to Katane and Komanos to command another troop and head to Taormina. Akhaeus and Dugga would follow with a force of eight thousand infantry and archers to support them and send small groups to harass Hypsaeus' diminished forces without engaging in full battle.

On the ground vacated by the enemy, weapons and body armour were collected, as well as the catapults, ballistas and siege equipment Hypsaeus had brought with him. In the panic Hypsaeus had left two standards, an Aquila and an orb with the figure of Victoria, as well as a banner hanging on a horizontal bar attached to a lance showing two sheaves of wheat around two swords. Upon arriving back in Enna with the spoils, Younis ordered them to be hoisted in various locations in or near the main square with a broken chain affixed to each.

Chapter 22

One week after the victory over Hypsaeus, the assembly met again, this time to celebrate the coronation of Younis as King of Sicilia. As a favourable omen, a special crown was forged on the rock platform outside the Temple of Demeter below the citadel. The diadem was crafted out of thin intricately-designed gold sheets, onto which wild berries and olive twigs were placed for the occasion. In the amphitheatre, the main stage and stairs were decked with sheaves of barley, wheat and wreaths of trailing ivy and many-coloured wild flowers.

Of all the liberated slaves, none was more respected and advanced in age than Abimilki. Past eighty years old, as a child he had seen the great Haniba'al. Later, as a youth, he had fought in the general's last battles. Selected to lead the coronation, he walked in the procession holding aloft the basket with the diadem. Behind him followed men and women who were prominent figures in the revolt, surrounded by a group of twelve children decked with garlands of flowers. Like a gracious priest, Abimilki raised his voice in prayer.

"We are your people, Great Goddess," he intoned. "In your honour we celebrate this occasion and give gratitude for what you have helped us to bring about. Mother of all, shelter those who perished in this endeavour in your gentle fold and grant them eternal life. Mother of all and supplier of bounteous plenty, shower your blessings upon us and upon this man and his fighters. Source of gods and mortals, all-fertile and all-destroying, help us to anchor the eternal world into our own. Immortal, blessed, crowned with every grace, deep-bosomed Earth, sweet grower of flowers, grasses and grains, high flyer who brings the god of nurturing rains, of the sun, around you are the beauteous stars, eternal and divine, Blessed Goddess, hear the prayers of your children, draw near and bless all of us your supplicants and this man who will carry your words and carry out your wishes. Protect him and his helpers, extend to them your strength and sustenance, and inspire them with knowledge and wisdom."

Abimilki placed the diadem on the head of Younis and kneeled in gratitude, while the assembly erupted in cheers and adulation. Younis held Abimilki's hand and asked him to stand up, embraced him and expressed his respect. "You do not need to kneel before me," he whispered to him, "I should be the one to show deference to your age and wisdom." One by one, all the notables and others young and old came up to the platform to greet Younis and pledge obeisance, bowing first and embracing him or kissing him on the cheek, and some kneeling and kissing his hand. It was a long while before he could speak amid the joyous tumult.

Younis stepped forth, raised the studded cane in his right hand, and gave thanks to the assembly for the honour bestowed upon him, humbled to receive their full trust, he told them, he would strive to be worthy of it. He declared in acknowledgement that the victory truly belonged to them and that the challenges in days ahead would be more arduous as they begin to build a society based upon justice. In honour of his homeland and its king who last challenged Roma, he proclaimed a wish to add Antiochos to Younis Basilius as his title. He also announced that soon he intended to publicly celebrate his marriage to Elissar, who would become their queen, to assist in fulfilling their aspirations for a better future for their children in a liberated land. The assembly cheered and chanted the names of Younis and Elissar.

Younis then laid down before the assembly the precepts to be applied for all subjects in the new dominion of Sicilia.

"We are all one," he started by saying, "those liberated from bondage, those farming the land and those grazing the sheep and cattle. Slavery comes in different forms and did not fall only on those who were in bondage after capture or sale. You the herders and shepherds who joined us were equally subjected to injustice, left in abject poverty while the landowners exploited you to feed their greed. You, the farmers on our side, without your unremitting labour the richness of this land and the plenty it gives back in return would be left to go barren. Henceforth these measures and statutes will govern all the people in this dominion:

That all humans who breathe are endowed with the same rights and duties;

That the land and properties of this dominion belong to the whole of the people as one;

That cultivated land will be divided among those willing to undertake the labour of husbandry, three hundred feet each side for every person in each family, who will give a quarter of their output for the prosperity of the kingdom and the needs of its army, the rest of which they are allowed to use or barter as determined by their needs;

That the herders of sheep and cattle have the right to adequate habitation and tracts of land to graze their herds, and work hand in hand with the farmers to ensure the livelihood of both, a quarter of what the herders produce to be given for the welfare of the kingdom and supply of its army;

That women, as heirs of our Great Goddess on earth and the source of future generations, should receive their due and possess in every respect the same rights and duties as all others;

That those engaged in the arts, crafts, metalwork, masonry and the other skills, are entitled to organise into eranoi for the advancement of their respective trades and the welfare of the people;

That those who worked in mansions anywhere on the island remain in their mansions and henceforth manage them for the common benefit, and as needed share them with others;

That the coins minted for transactions are in no way to be used for hoarding or making one person richer and more powerful than another;

SLAVE KING

That no one shall gain advantage or power over another by use of buying or selling or by acquiring more property than is allowed to everyone else;

That no one shall be left to want for food or clothing.

These laws, to which more will be added as required, as well as such laws as agreed to by communal decisions, are to be written down and distributed for all to know, as guides to be applied by governors and assemblies in all corners of this Kingdom of Free Sicilia."

He then called on the people to make this a day of celebration and remembrance. Music played and the people rejoiced in dance and song, with festivities spilling into the streets. The entire city and its mansions celebrated with banquets, drinking and merriment that lasted into the night.

The next day, Younis ordered the minting of four issues of brass coins for use in daily transactions and two in gold for trade outside the island. Three of the brass coins showed his diademed head on the obverse. On the reverse, one had a winged thunderbolt representing the god of rain, the second a bunch of grapes as a sign of the land's plenty and the third the club of Herakles to denote strength and determination. For the fourth brass coin, the obverse had the figure of Demeter and the reverse an ear of barley. The two gold issues, melted from captured bounty or otherwise acquired, showed a similar obverse as the first three brass coins. On its reverse, the first featured the figure of winged Nike wearing a crown. On the second, a soldier stood atop a pile of armour holding a spear in commemoration of their victories.

Chapter 23

Lamia and her friends were at a loss at first how best to include their traditions in the wedding, to preserve its emblematic meanings. On this occasion, the details were many— how the bride was to be prepared according to the customs of their homeland and how the groom's friends would ready him, what presents to offer the bride and groom on their special day, and what else was expected to ensure esteem for everyone present before and during the ceremony. The younger women had no experience of such celebrations, having been deprived of them during their enslavement or were too young to remember them well. In Enna and elsewhere, marriages between slaves, even citizens and freed slaves, were prohibited and considered illegal. Only two older women knew enough about these traditions. Tabiba and another woman from the Cinna estate, Tatia, having both been married in the old country, were now the only resort. Since people did not have normal families during their enslavement, it was natural for them to feel they could take on the roles of relatives on such occasions. Lamia, Nara, Mikhaila and other young women acted as sisters and nieces, Tatia was an aunt, Tabiba was the mother, Kleon and Nilos and other fighters were brothers and cousins.

Tabiba, Tatia and the younger women sat in a circle. Tabiba went through recalling a list of preparations related to the bride and groom and other customs. Tabiba mentioned two artifacts of special meaning in their homeland, which distinguished the occasion, but which required time to prepare. One was the bridal dress. The other was a special honeymoon blanket. Both were to be embroidered in a particular style—the dress to make the bride look splendidly worthy of her family and country and the blanket for the nuptial bed as an auspicious symbol of future plenty. To complete these articles for their queen in time, she told the women, they had to organise and work efficiently together as a group, which in a way would then be an example to be emulated for future weddings. In the two weeks remaining before the ceremony, they dedicated themselves to completing the dress and the blanket, four or sometimes six gathering to embroider them at the same time working from the edges to the centre. Tabiba drew a detailed design for the blanket on a sheet of papyrus. Two lengths of ivory-coloured woollen yarn were stitched to make the width required for a large bed. Starting at the borders, she outlined a framing box with angular stripes of alternating colours, red, gold and green or grey. For the main panels, Tabiba traced an intricate pattern mostly of multi-coloured flowers and spikes of wheat. For the central seam it was particularly challenging to coordinate the alternating triangles on the borders, stitched in three colours of red, yellow and charcoal. She gave the women the option of changing colours, still telling them that, like green for fertility, red and yellow were particularly meaningful in that they symbolised happiness, harmony, vigour and prosperity. Not to worry too much about exact colours as long as they were close, she added, as it was part of the essence of such a blanket to have various shades that added subtlety and represented an authentic natural quality. As encouragement, Tabiba told them that their working together to produce the embroidered design was in itself a *baraka*, in that the weaving of needlework using their own hands together, making sure their patterns meet, sometimes even passing the embroidering thread from one to another, would instill a soul blessing and good omen into the blanket that will last a lifetime and be felt by the persons using it.

Tatia knew how to apply the *kufra* to hands and feet, and had produced a supply of it. Remembering the *hinna* tree from which it is made, she had scoured the wilderness until she found it and collected its leaves and seeds, which she often used to treat infections and various ailments and even ingested its liquid to ease her joints and help her to sleep. She said she would be happy to apply the *kufra*, as they called it, with the other women present to watch. In the morning before the wedding day, the mother, aunt and sisters took the embroidered dress and congregated at the Antigenes mansion for the application of *kufra* to Elissar's hands and feet. Elissar was happy to have it on her skin since she understood its ritual function and its connection to the cycles of nature, and had heard of legends about the goddess Tanīt, their ʿAnat, adorning herself to celebrate the victory of Baʿal over Mot and the return of fertility. Elissar told Tatia beforehand that she wanted the designs to be simple and sparingly decorated. She sat patiently, surrounded by the women, as Tatia outlined the flower and geometric designs and then carefully applied the *kufra* paste using a slim cone shaped to spread thin lines on the hands and feet. Elissar was asked to avoid using water to wash until the evening, when the dried paste could be scrubbed off with a cloth and olive oil spread gently on the designs to protect the colour on the skin. The next day, Elissar was elated to notice with strange fascination that the reddish brown over her hands and feet had deepened and that the edges of her toes were particularly accented in dark red.

In the morning of the wedding day, both Elissar and Younis were bathed, perfumed and adorned by their friends. At the assigned time in mid afternoon, Younis stood outside the mansion, in a simple ivory-white tunic and light purple hip-cloak, surrounded by Nilos, Kleon and other men, his long hair combed and his beard trimmed, waiting until Elissar walked out with Tabiba and Lamia at her side. Elissar was wearing the dress the women had embroidered for her, radiant in its colours, and on her head had the peach-coloured beaded scarf her mother had given her. Younis took Elissar's dyed hand and they started their walk on the pathway toward the Temple of Demeter, the crowd on both sides showering soft leaves and flower petals, the aromas rising as they stepped on the strewn flowers. A single flutist played ahead of Lamia and Nilos accompanied by twelve children, six boys and six girls, carrying bouquets of flowers. All senses were awakened on this short walk to the temple. More than merely physical, it was a journey that augured hope and good fortune. As they approached the temple an unexpected cloud sprinkled a light drizzle and passed, reminding everyone of what Tabiba mentioned a few days before. She said that if rain—even just a few droplets—fell, the two people to be wedded can look forward to heaven's help and blessing in ensuring productivity for the land to be tilled and the home to be built.

Most of the people were already crowded around the great rock in anticipation as Elissar and Younis ascended to the platform where Abimilki, who as elder assumed the function of priest, stood in front of a stone pedestal decorated with wild flowers and olive branches, a small tray on it. The children and the two witnesses stood behind them as Abimilki, after a short silence, commenced to say:

"We meet here on this sacred ground to unite two people in the salve of marriage, to join them heart to heart in eternal joy, to make their fields grow fertile and their gardens bring forth bounteous fruits to sweeten their lives. May their desire to be together give them the spirit and strength to meet all challenges that life will bring."

He held out the small tray with two thin gold rings, from which Elissar chose one ring and Younis took the other. Abimilki paused briefly, what seemed a long time, then pronounced the vows:

"Younis, son of Maryam and Aqbar of Afamia, parents who in spirit are part of this blessing, do you take Elissar as your wife, to treasure her, honour and support her in this world?"

"Yes, I promise to treasure, honour and support Elissar in this world," answered Younis. Abimilki repeated the question twice and received the answer "Yes I do" twice.

"Elissar, daughter of Thubaba and Tabnit of Qart Ḥadašt, parents who in spirit are part of this blessing, do you take Younis as your husband, to treasure him, honour and support him in this world?"

"Yes, I promise to treasure, honour and support Younis in this world," answered Elissar. Abimilki repeated the question twice and received the answer "Yes I do" twice. Younis held Elissar's left hand, slipped the ring onto her third finger. Younis kissed Elissar on the forehead, and then she held Younis' left hand, put the ring onto his third finger and kissed him on the forehead.

Abimilki turned to the two witnesses, Lamia and Nilos, and asked each of them "Have you heard and do you verify this pledge," to which each answered "I have heard and verify it." By partaking in this special gathering with their friends, Lamia and Nilos were thinking of themselves as well in solemn togetherness that will stay with them as a harbinger of their own in days ahead.

"With her blessing and protection, mother of the universe, mistress of all the elements, the one who controls the shining heights of heaven and the sun and the health-giving rains and winds of earth, I declare you husband and wife, king and queen. Surpassing your many trials and tribulations you stand here united to banish all past strangeness and to bring happiness into our midst. Under your reign, may the earth grow fertile, the sheepfolds multiply, may there be plants for nourishment, may there be wheat for our bread, may the rivers flow more freely, the fish multiply in the nets, may the birds sing on trees and amid the grasses, the deer and wild goats multiply in the forests, may the orchards bring forth honey and wine, the fields grow high with lettuce and cress, may the meadows be filled with sheaves and mounds of grain."

As Abimilki ended, the crowd standing under the platform cheered and a group of women started celebratory ululations.

"We sisters of the bride in joy we stand still," intonated the lead ululator, followed by the loud high-pitched ululating of the group.

"Out of full silver cups our mouths we fill," sang the lead ululator, followed by the trilling from other women.

"We were strangers who recently met," intoned the lead singer, with the other women ululating in response.

"And now we're relatives forever set," retorted the lead ululator, with the other women responding with long ululations. And as the procession moved, she sang out:

"Open the doors and let in the guest,
Tonight, tonight the lovers reach their quest."

Elissar and Younis felt joyful as the women escorting them continued trilling. As their procession ascended the hill toward the gate, it was surprised by a line of fighters, fifteen on each side of the road, the men of Kleon and Nilos, raising their swords and shields, who started beating swords against shields as the animated crowd approached, their punctuated rhythmic thumping and chanting reverberating across the hills.

"Where did the lioness queen go to seek?" one side shouted as swords banged against shields more loudly.

"Into the dense forest she ran deep," intoned the other side in return.

"The lion king was utterly dazed."

"With her manifest beauty he stood amazed."

"To the warm den the two then scurry."

"To raise their cubs and live all merry."

Each shout was followed by sustained clanging with swords and shields, after which one fighter raised his voice in question:

"What did the fisherman net from the deep?"

"A precious pearl he'll forever keep," answered a fighter on the other side, with other fighters continuing to bang against the shields.

"What did two hawks do when they met flying?" improvised another fighter.

"They perched on a cliff edge to nest their hatchling," answered one from the other side, followed by punctuated thumping with swords against shields.

The warriors continued their rhythmic beats as they escorted the procession until it reached the banquet hall entrance. A group

of men and women took over to receive them, the men lifting Younis above their heads and other men and women carrying Elissar
in a chair to be seated at the head table for the evening of feasting,
wine, beer, foods and good words. As more people filed in, a group
of ten men and women sprang up into an impromptu *khigga* dance
in the centre of the hall, a dance harking back to the ancient celebrations of a plenteous harvest. They formed a semicircle with the
lead dancer in front waving a cane with bells, while the rest kept
up by treading in rhythmic steps to the tune played by the flutist
and drummer, one leg forward then back, the other leg forward
and back, then accentuated by a hop and stomp. As more people
joined in the dance, holding each other's hands, they formed a circle with the lead dancer in the centre flying gracefully in skillful
twists and turns, stomping with his feet, measuring out the melody.
After the moment late in the evening when friends coaxingly led
the bride and groom to the bedroom, celebrants continued their
joyful feasting through the night and into the early morning until
the sun's rising.

Chapter 24

Three girls and three boys were sitting cross-legged in a circle on a grassy patch at the edge of a cobbled alley. Their clothing was oddly different, some more richly attired and others in worn plain tunics. One boy was flinging objects in the air when Elissar walked by with Lamia. Elissar and Lamia stopped to watch. The children looked up.

"What are you playing, my dears?"

"It's a game with knuckle bones. We play it in different ways," answered a girl who looked about seven. Elissar could see the five bones on the ground, obviously made from the pastern bones of some animal, probably sheep or goat.

"What's your name?" Elissar asked the girl.

"My name is Zoë."

"Whose daughter are you?"

"My mother is Sosia. My father is Hermon."

"It's good you're enjoying playing together."

"We are friends. It's different now," said the older boy whom she recognised as Markus, the son of the imprisoned Trimalcio.

"So, what are the rules of the game?"

"It depends. Sometimes we throw the bones and see how many each of us can catch on the back of the hand. The one who catches most wins," Zoë explained.

"Isn't that difficult with your little hands?"

"I spread my fingers and catch more than one," said the youngest, Laila, whom Elissar thought was the daughter of Munim and Tania. "But I like to play ball. We need more to play a game."

"And do you know how to make a ball?"

"Zoë knows," answered Laila, pointing to Zoë. "She once made a really beautiful ball. She stuffed a cloth and then stitched it with all sorts of coloured thread, red and green and other colours."

"And what are you playing now?"

"We hold the bones with two hands and throw them up. When they fall to the ground, we count the sides. Whoever gets the highest number wins," Markus explained.

"Count the sides? How? Show me."

Markus threw up the bones, and pointed out the different sides and their values.

"There are four ways the bones fall, and each side is given a different number. We add the numbers and see who has the most."

"Can you all add?"

"No, we can't do that well. I only know what the numbers mean, but can't always add them correctly, but we try. Markus knows. He's the one who counts, and he's teaching us how to do that too," said a plainly dressed boy who looked about the same age as Markus.

"We trust Markus because he doesn't always win," Zoë chuckled.

Elissar and Lamia laughed with her, and Markus smiled.

"Enjoy the game," Lamia said, and they bid the children goodbye.

"I can almost read your mind," Lamia said aside as they walked away.

"Yes, but will they be friends for long? Why wasn't it possible to have been friends before and why not friends forever? I was also thinking about the boy who said he couldn't count very well."

"What do you think should be done for the children?"

"It used to be that the landowners had tutors for their children but the children of slaves had little chance to learn, unless some parents had knowledge and time to teach them. The best thing now would be to have all the tutors in one place or close by so they meet with the children together to teach various subjects and skills."

Elissar set about the next day to choose a place. She sent out messengers to call those who tutored before or had the skills to help.

Elissar sat as more than a queen and did not think of her title as an empty honour to be used for pretence. She knew her work would be unlike anything else she had done before. It was not enough, she remarked to Lamia, for Younis to say in the assembly that women had the same rights and duties. The women must demonstrate that truth now more than ever since their own lives depended on making sure the new dominion survived. Elissar went about daily asking the women to see what they could contribute and what different women thought and wanted to do, discussions that started to take on new purpose. Most urgent was another pressing task, how to procure, prepare and distribute the supply of quantities of food and material for the increasing number of troops. Elissar asked Lamia if she could take over organising this work to relieve the men. Kleon's men, having lived in the forest, had developed the skills to prepare nutritious food and were adept at washing clothes and keeping their camp clean, but their time and efforts were increasingly taxed by the demand of training others to fight. Lamia agreed to find a place and recruit a group of women and men to prepare what supplies and rations of dried and preserved foods were to be loaded when the troops go out.

For other women, it was not enough to help the metal workers and carpenters in weapon making and other war preparations. Some were keen to join the fight, she heard, perhaps as a separate contingent, and she could see that several of them would make good fighters. To find a leader for such a troop seemed difficult in Enna, so she decided to go out on a search in outlying estates and towns. For more than a week, it became her daily routine to take a carriage with Lamia and two attendants, with them three mounted guards, for the purpose of scouring the countryside to check on living conditions and also search for women fighters.

It was toward the end of one such trip to an estate on the eastern side of Lake Pergusa that she found her. Elissar was told of a woman called Nara, who descended from the Samarti tribes and a long line of warriors. She had been brought to the island as a small girl and had since proved to be very troublesome, and often punished by her mistress and the overseer. People told Elissar that when news of the revolt reached them from Enna, Nara led a group that went into the mansion and arrested the landlord and mistress, and then the guards and overseer. Nara had tried to control the crowd, but could not prevent them from clubbing the landowner and the overseer.

Upon arrival in the mansion, Elissar immediately noticed a woman standing against a wooden fence at the edge of a field, tall and strongly built, a spritely demeanour accented by unusual dark reddish hair.

"I am Elissar, the wife of Younis," Elissar said as she approached Nara.

Nara bowed a bit and asked permission to give Elissar an embrace. "This revolt is what we have all been waiting and searching for to lead us out of our miseries."

"I have been searching for you too. I heard of what you have done."

"It was what needed to be done. I wish I could do more."

"Let's talk about that." It didn't take long for Elissar to convince Nara to return with her to Enna.

It was by another coincidence one day that from her carriage Elissar saw Kleon returning to Enna from one of his raiding escapades. And there a few riders back she sighted a woman who looked slim and sprightly, fully armed, a bow slung on her shoulder. How could I not have thought of looking right here? Elissar said to herself. She sent a messenger to ask Kleon to arrange for the woman to meet her. Mikhaila appeared the next morning, unarmed and unhelmeted. Her profuse black hair looked like a bush, and her brown eyes had a hint of green, her dark skin and her features evoking shades of lands farther east. Elissar inquired about her origin. Mikhaila told her that she had been born to a tribe of desert nomads south of Tadmor, and was captured, barely ten years of age, by a band of armed men along with two other children at a water hole as they were carrying jugs back to their encampment.

They talked for a while before Elissar found the moment to broach the subject. "I would like us to be friends. You must come to visit me often," Elissar started. "I called you to ask because several women say they are keen to share in fighting with the men, like you. They want to see themselves winning battles, not stay behind and maybe later blame fate. You joined Kleon to do that, I'm sure. Would you agree to help train a group of women? A few gladiators and archers can be asked for additional help at the beginning to prepare the women in the skills of using defensive weapons to guard the towns and lands. It would be a great sight that raises the spirits to see a body of women on horseback ride into the field as a force of their own with bows and arrows and swords sheathed at the ready."

"We are descended from people who lived in tents and led armies," answered Mikhaila. "In my childhood I still remember as if today we used to huddle around the coals to listen to my grandmother telling us about Šammīrām, Ḥatšepsut and the goddesses Sakhmet and ʿAnat, and other great women and their feats, those too who fought at the head of armies and conquered lands. It would be a great honour to do what you ask."

This agreed, they sat heart-to-heart like sisters. They felt close, as if they had known each other from childhood. Elissar told Mikhaila about her young memories of Qart Ḥadašt, how she was separated from her mother, and how she was brought to Enna and met Younis.

"Is there anyone to whom you are attached?" Elissar asked casually. Mikhaila smiled, and a slight blush came to her face.

"No. I don't think of that, something far from my mind. It is difficult to find one to trust after all that happened."

"Maybe you will. Younis and I found each other. You are a friend now, so I can tell you. Only Younis knows. I told him yesterday.

I am with child," Elissar said. Mikhaila stood up and moved toward Elissar, embraced and kissed her on the cheek.

"It makes me happiest to know there will be others of you. I love the children here and often play with them. They cheer my spirit. How beautiful it will be to have a little boy or girl with you to feel like family again."

In her first year as queen Elissar worked to start plans for the benefit of their kingdom and was always on the lookout for ways to build a community. It was then that Mikhaila and Nara became commanders in the army of Younis in Sicilia.

Chapter 25

After the defeat of Hypsaeus and then, in succession, the praetors Manlius, Lentulus and Flaccus, it seemed the empire was leaving Sicilia in peace for a while. Rebel forces had chased the commanders of Roma into disgraceful retreat, destroying their armies, killing many of their soldiers both in battle and in retreat and taking their weapons and other booty. As they collected more weapons and supplies, the rebel army grew in number to more than a hundred thousand. The senate in Roma did not send any legions for more than three years, not for lack of desire to do so, but out of fear of suffering another humiliation, surprised at the numbers that had joined the uprising and shown unexpected skills in battle. Roma was biding its time. It would surely send a large force once it had overcome difficulties elsewhere and found ways to recruit enough troops to suppress other revolts. Roma's armies had been smarting from constant attacks by the bold shepherd Viriato in Iberia, who waged a fearsome war of surprise raids and ambushes against them following the atrocious massacres committed by Servius Sulpicius Galba. Even after Roma paid traitors to kill Viriato, forebodings of more resistance persisted as unrest continued among the Lusitani and other tribes. The Numantine War was still raging, and other uprisings flared up, inspired by the success in Sicilia, in the mines of Attikís and in Athênai, in Delos and elsewhere. At Sinuessa in Campania several thousand slaves had to be subdued at great cost in men and munitions.

Most cities in Sicilia did not require direct conquest. News of the revolt traveled fast across the island, leading more slaves, herders and farmers to rise up in great masses almost everywhere. Some cities surrendered to the emissaries sent by Younis, while in other cities the slaves overpowered semi-abandoned garrisons, arrested magistrates, and dispatched messages of allegiance. To most cities, Younis either went himself or sent one of his commanders to organise the appointment of governors, to apply the new laws, and to ensure appropriate defences and training. In cities that had gladiators, training those able to fight was done without requiring the deployment of troops from Enna. One city remained a problem, Missina, the port in the northeastern corner of the island across from the peninsula, which was supported by a large fleet.

Among the places that put up resistance was the port of Akragas on the southern coast. Kleon had laid siege to Akragas, but its walls were strong and a galley commander off the coast prevented the city's surrender. Younis decided to take more troops, with additional catapults and towers, and join Kleon in the siege.

It eventually turned out to be an almost farcical affair. The city's magistrate and its council were fully aware that they were surrounded by the countryside under rebel control and a population that could not be relied on to remain loyal. The large number of slaves within its walls seemed to be compliant but could turn at any moment. On the day of his arrival, Younis sent a message to the magistrate to demand the city's surrender. He informed him that the city would thus avoid unnecessary destruction, that their lives, those of other landowners and the garrison would be saved. When the magistrate and council refused, one of the rebels by the name of Origen, who is adept in the literary arts and had acted in comedies by Menander and Plautus, suggested having a play he had written performed outside the walls to help change their minds. Though certainly an unusual approach in vying for a city's surrender, still Younis thought this to be worth trying, even if nothing came of it except a bit of entertainment in an extreme situation. As Origen made preparations, a message was sent to the city on the third day asking the magistrate to congregate with landowners and citizens that afternoon at the southwest corner of the city walls, which overlooks the Valley of Temples and in particular the amphitheatre.

Origen and the actors he chose were ready, most of the rebel troops attending in the amphitheatre and the magistrate along with a crowd of landowners, citizens and slaves in position to watch from the ramparts. Origen had chosen his masks to distinguish slaves from soldiers and landowners, as well as children from older men. For children Origen used shorter men as actors and had them wear masks showing young features, and female roles were acted by women who accompanied the rebel army. The play began with a horrid battle scene in which soldiers slaughtered men and dragged women and children away. In a plot thick with turns and surprises, a central element is a tragic love story, where the young son of a landlord, enamoured of a slave girl, struggles with the problem of how to bring about an honourable resolution. In an affectionate meeting the youth pledges his eternal allegiance to the young woman and promises to seek her freedom and their marriage. In ugly contrast, the young man's father casts lascivious glances at the slave girl and gives vent to his desire in a degrading scene in which the young woman is beaten into submission and faints as the father ravishes her. Later the young man learns of the rape. Seeing the visible scars on her face and body, he rushes toward his father to denounce the ugly deed. A struggle ensues when the father maintains his right as the owner to pick the fruit anytime he wants, then he slaps the youth and demands his compliance, the action and dialogue dramatising the clash between the young man's honourable feelings and the father's stone-hearted response. A struggle ensues, and the young man impulsively stabs the father in the chest and neck, a scene filled with gruesome details. Origen had devised a large bladder filled with blood placed around the neck and chest of the actor who played the father, so that when the son inserts the knife blood spurts out into a long pool of red all over the stage. In another scene before the end, the tables are turned, the children and adult slaves arrest the landowners and soldiers and secure them in chains, some on the ground grovelling and begging for mercy, the children holding them down with wooden hooks and stepping on their necks. At the end, a man of horrible visage, obviously old, his long hair white, his mask with mouth aghast and eyes round, delivers an epilogue about the evils of slavery and cruelties of landowners who enjoy such practices, and concludes by reciting the lessons learned from this spectacle that those who once had committed brutalities and inequities still have a chance to repent so the world can be made just again.

It is uncertain what influence the play had on the magistrate and his council. The magistrate, his council and the soldiers of course saw the additional siege equipment brought against them and the troops ready to scale the walls. The play, however, moved the slaves inside the walls to action. Hundreds of them grabbed what tools, clubs, small knives, and anything else at hand to use as weapons, torched the magistrate's house, rampaged through the streets, then entered the temple and put up barricades against the door. They sent an ultimatum to the magistrate demanding that he surrender the city. The magistrate then met the centurion to inform him that further resistance was futile, and advised a course of action whereby the garrison and others who chose to leave would take boats to the warship at anchor. With this agreed, he sent a message to Younis accepting the terms of surrender.

In this fourth year of the rebellion, Roma sent another army led by Lucius Calpurnius Piso. First reports reached Enna from Komanos that six legions had landed and were advancing from Missina to Taormina. By then, rebel forces numbered more than a hundred and fifty thousand, of which more than half could be deployed for this battle. When they arrived to find Piso entrenched in his siege of the city, Younis and Kleon decided not to engage the legions immediately. Instead, they pitched camp several miles west down from the heights of Mylai. From there, Kleon launched several surprise attacks on the enemy camp and siege formations, about one hundred of his cavalry at each point, with groups of archers in support on the flanks, one led by Dugga and another by Mikhaila. These skirmishes debilitated Piso's forces, and forced him to abandon his original plans to breach the walls. At the same time, they left him uncertain as to whether the rebel forces intended to surround him. He decided to avert the danger by advancing to attack, as became obvious from his preparations. That night, another diversion was devised. Nara and Yousif, with help from herders, collected all the sheep, goats and cattle they could find. To each animal they tied a torch. It was a long line, and when the torches were lit it appeared in the dark night as if the troops were moving toward the north and northwest. Piso must have thought they had decided either to cut off his supply lines or attack him from the north. It was in that direction, the lights sighted at night, that Piso moved his army the next day believing he was pursuing the rebels. Instead, Dugga, Nilos, Nara and Mikhaila had taken up positions in the forests and passes where Piso least expected. Choosing their point of attack carefully, they divided Piso's infantry into three pieces. It was more than the superior numbers and determination of the rebels that put Piso's infantry to flight. Dugga turned what carts they had into chariots with weapons, affixing long sharp blades to the wheels. With these, his archers plowed through enemy lines, dismembering many and wreaking havoc. Mikhaila was even more inventive. Helped by herders, she collected a large pack of wild dogs that had been caught and trained and unleashed them at the right moment to bite into legs and arms and otherwise spread alarm among Piso's soldiers. When Piso's cavalry turned to meet other surprise attacks, Kleon outflanked it and put to rout all who were not killed on the spot. Piso could not even return to his camp near Taormina, and was forced to make a full retreat to Missina.

For more than three years after this battle, Sicilia would not come under attack by the legions. It was not until the seventh year of the Sicilian kingdom of Younis that Roma sent its largest army yet.

Chapter 26

Fresh from his efficiently severe inquiry against friends of the murdered Tiberius Gracchus, Publius Rupilius had landed with eight legions in the port of Missina and advanced to besiege Taormina. Younis and Kleon had been unable to take Missina from the start. Roma had made sure to retain its hold on it as the northeastern bridgehead to the peninsula, backed by a strong fleet in the straits. It was feared that Missina would remain a launching point for future attacks on the island. In retrospect, it was indeed a grave strategic error for the rebels not to have made every possible effort to take the port and remove this danger. Instead, they opted not to press their advantages when Roma's defeated armies under Hypsaeus, then Manlius and after him Lentulus, Flaccus and Piso had been defeated and retreated to the protection of Missina. Missina remained a sealed box. It was the rebels' weak point, and now it was too late to do anything about it.

Urgent messages dispatched from Komanos in Taormina did not reach Younis in time because neither he nor Kleon were still in Enna. The first messengers to arrive found Nilos in command of a small force, and he could do nothing except to relay the message to Younis. Two weeks before, Younis had received reports of trouble in Panormos, the port city in the north, and news that it had been attacked by a fleet anchored offshore. Younis feared that ancient Ziz would become a second base for Roma to move forces into the island's interior. The messengers from Nilos reached Younis and Kleon after they had taken back control of Panormos and were preparing to return to Enna. Its re-conquest proved to be an empty victory, and had necessitated leaving behind a larger garrison. It became obvious that the threat was exaggerated since the fleet consisted of only four triremes. Worse, the small fleet might

have landed at Panormos to divert attention from the main assault at Missina. Taormina was in threat of being taken, the fate of
Komanos unknown. Rupilius obviously wanted to continue his advance toward Katane and then move to besiege Enna. What Younis
had wanted to avoid from the outset, to be forced to defend Enna
against a siege, now seemed inevitable. Younis and Kleon decided
that the only option to meet this grave threat was to reach Enna
quickly, and for Kleon to go out in cavalry sorties to intercept advance enemy forces to try to disrupt and delay their movement.

In Taormina, the situation was critical as Komanos waited for
instructions. He needed reinforcements for sure, but would Younis
and Kleon decide to send the main rebel force to face Rupilius in
the field? Should he withdraw from the city? To leave Rupilius unchallenged would only increase his chances and bolster his numbers with local allies and citizen recruits as he moved from one
city to the next. Before the siege could be sealed, Komanos ordered
elements of his cavalry to go out in forays to harass the advancing
legions and burn their supplies. Meanwhile, many freed slaves in
the surrounding villages and mansions had converged to take shelter inside the city walls. Komanos could not possibly have prevented the influx, but he also did not consider the potential dangers in
allowing the entry of many strangers.

Among those coming into the city were two exploratores dis-
guised as farmers whose task was to locate places most suited for
breaching the fortifications, using fire signals to communicate with
legion commanders. This information was critical for Rupilius as
he waited for the additional siege equipment he required to arrive
from the port. The two spies, who called themselves Castos and
Sarafi, claimed when asked to have come from Kilikia and Syria.
Once inside, they stayed together in a shed not far from the walls.
The city was in general unreceptive to control by the rebels, having
previously made favourable pacts with Roma that granted special
benefits to the citizen population, so only allegiance from the freed

slaves could be guaranteed. The two men had little trouble in establishing contact with citizen collaborators on lists given to them and in relaying useful particulars, often pretending to be defenders as they surveyed the walls. In addition to locating weak spots in the fortifications, they were to communicate and send helpful signals one day before the first assault.

Komanos repelled several breaches in the wall, but shuttling back and forth between these points only weakened his position. Finally, a major incursion from the western wall overwhelmed the defenses and determined the outcome. Komanos and his men put up strong resistance, attempting to delay legion soldiers by building barricades to obstruct alleys and defending with archers. Their numbers were just too small to resist the onslaught. After two weeks of siege, along with severe shortages in food and supplies, this breach forced Komanos to decide on his own to abandon the city. His only option was to attempt a breakout with his remaining cavalry from what he thought was the best spot out of the southern wall. Riding at the head of his cavalry, Komanos spurted out in an arrow formation, determined to die fighting if he could not penetrate enemy lines, or at least to give the chance for some of his fighters to escape. He succeeded at first in dispersing several Roman units, but almost at the edge of safety beyond enemy lines his troop was showered with a dark cloud of javelins and arrows. His horse was struck, and as it fell into a ditch Komanos slammed with full force against a rock, knocking him unconscious.

Chapter 27

Komanos woke to find his hands tied behind his back and a yoke around his neck. He was pinned by chains to a post outside a large tent. His head was still bleeding, and on both sides of his face, his blonde hair was encrusted with blood. He was captured as he lay in the ditch and did not recover consciousness until he felt the soldiers tying him up. *How many made it through?* was the first thought that crossed his mind.

Rupilius ordered that Komanos be brought to his tent. Tall and brawny, unhelmeted, Rupilius' round face revealed pockmarks under a trimmed beard. His deep-set brown eyes and a fold below his chin suggested that he was more overweight than one would assume from the tight leather breastplate and body armour. His apparent purpose was to extract information from Komanos, though he also seemed curious to know more about the character of these rebels who had humiliated other commanders sent by Roma.

"Here's the man, Kleon's brother," Rupilius said, as much to himself as to Komanos.

"I am Komanos of Kilikia. I am proud to call Kleon my brother in blood and in arms."

"He will be brought to heel very soon, just as you are now."

"Don't think you'll ever succeed in doing that. I did not expect to be alive. Your spies will never be able to lure another collaborator with gold coins to betray him as you did here. Kleon is much too clever for your tricks. Whatever happens, we will fight to the death."

"If you want to escape the agonies of the crucifix you will tell me what I want to know and declare your allegiance to me before the people."

"You mean I will be left to rot in your prisons instead of receiving immediate death. Why would I pledge allegiance to such oppression?" Rupilius did not respond but instead asked:

"So you will answer my questions?"

"I am standing here in front of you."

"What number does Kleon command in cavalry?"

"There are many, you cannot imagine how many, who will give their lives and never surrender."

"Where are the rebel forces hiding on the road?"

"They are here and there and everywhere. They will appear and disappear."

"I'll give you a last chance to answer. How many men are defending Enna?"

"There are countless men, and there are women too. They will make Enna impossible for any army to take."

"You mock us with your replies," turning to his lieutenants. Rupilius continued, "We shall pull the answers from his mouth on the wheel. Take him away. "

Komanos was standing next to a table with a bowl of fruit on it. He bent down to the bowl and picked up two apricots into his mouth, one he appeared to swallow whole and the second he kept lodged in his throat. He held his mouth shut, closed his eyes, bent his head down, and stopped his breathing. Rupilius noticed this action and moved closer to Komanos. The soldiers guarding Komanos attempted to open his mouth, to no avail. In less than two minutes, his colour changed and the weight of his body gave way. In another minute, he was lying motionless on the ground, sideways, his long blonde hair covering part of his face that had turned blue. Two soldiers bent down to examine the body, looked up to Rupilius to confirm the death.

Rupilius stood astonished at this self-killing.

"I cannot imagine anyone could do this," he said, turning to his lieutenant. "Here is a noble and brave man indeed. I hope not too many like him are left for us to fight." He asked the soldiers to remove the body and instructed them to give it a proper burial on high ground.

Chapter 28

Publius Rupilius was well aware that Enna was different from Taormina as he laid siege to it. His forces could not get as close to the fortifications here, and his attempts to find a weakness failed on every attempt. He could neither get his spies inside nor find traitors as he did elsewhere. His siege towers were unusable in this case, while the ballista and catapults were limited in application. The fortifications had been extended to the edges of the cliffs to prevent battering rams or siege towers from reaching anywhere close to the walls or the gate. Rupilius ordered several assaults on the southeastern escarpment using ramps and ladders, one at dawn and the last in the middle of the night. His men were decimated by showers of rocks and arrows. Rebel fighters had fashioned missiles filled with oil, larger ones made of hide and smaller ones using bladders, which they sent tumbling down to explode onto Roman ramps and ladders, to be followed by incendiary arrows that consumed men and equipment.

The rebel forces did not stop at defending their positions. Kleon, now grieving his brother's death, was moved to act even more fiercely. He went out on kill and burn sorties at the edges of the enemy camp, and in one instance targeted Roman supply stores, putting them to the torch. Rupilius could not figure out how Kleon managed to leave and return to the city with his cavalry. The shortages began to take their toll, so he sent bands of his men to the countryside to garner food and supplies only to discover that the farmers and shepherds had either moved away to distant locations or joined the rebel fighters in Enna with what supplies they had.

Even a victory in Enna would be sullied by knowing it was one achieved over slaves, no dignity or fame in that for a proconsul, thought Rupilius. He was not in danger of losing the battle, but he was well aware that a long unresolved siege or retreat or the appearance of one could be construed as a defeat. He dreaded reminding the senate of what had befallen the disgraced praetors before him: camps overrun, and in one case the praetor himself captured and killed. Rupilius was concerned how long it might take to achieve a successful breach or surrender, or whether he would have to abandon the siege if the depletion of his forces and supplies continued. It was autumn, and the coming cold would be yet another advantage to a city well-stocked with food and weapons. He finally opted for a different course to achieve the purpose and save face: a meeting with Younis. His emissary stood below the escarpment waiving a white flag until Kleon's men arrived to receive the message.

Younis was wary of a ruse, but agreed to meet Rupilius and sent a reply with conditions. To ensure safety, he notified Rupilius to meet him at the entrance to the Temple of Demeter, near the Great Rock, not far from the escarpment and in clear sight of the walls. Rupilius was to approach the place with no more than five guards. For his part Younis rode out with Nilos and four of Kleon's seasoned cavalrymen.

"So here is the man who has given us so much trouble," Rupilius greeted Younis almost wittily.

"Wish there would have been no need for such trouble if Roma had not persisted in enslaving people. I have myself come unarmed, though my guards are. I ask that you put aside your sword. We can sit there to speak," replied Younis, pointing to an outcrop about forty paces away.

Rupilius dismounted, removed his helmet and sword, undid his purple cloak and slung it onto the saddle. Without the helmet, Rupilius' pockmarks, the emblem of a victory in a different kind of battle, stood out clearly under his short beard. Younis was standing next to his horse, and started to walk toward the outcrop. Both men had a practical purpose to achieve, and there was no room for hostility or other sentiments. Rupilius had told his prefect that he wanted to remain calm and mask his unease at having to deal with a slave. It was nothing glorious for commanders of Roma's legions even to overcome and defeat slaves who rebel, believing them to be inferior in the values of humanity. It was certainly much more humiliating for their vain nobility to be confronted by the strength of those they wished to believe were below them, in this case a slave who had defeated several armies sent by Roma and shamed their commanders. But he had to do what was necessary to take the city.

"What is it that will make you leave Enna?" The proconsul asked abruptly as they reached the outcrop.

"You know very well that we can hold out in Enna for a long time, years if we so wish. Our water supply is endless, our food is secure. We have enough people to defend the city and take the battle to you. And winter is coming."

"All this may be true. We will wait. The senate has decided it will spare no effort to regain the whole of Sicilia. Most of the revolts that occupied us elsewhere have been subdued. The senate is determined to end this one. You have Enna, but other cities we have taken back. If I ask for more legions the senate will send them."

"Is not that exactly the problem that Roma will continue to face rebellions?"

"Tell me, what will make you leave Enna and end this situation?"

"Three things."

"Yes, what are they?"

"Those who wish to leave the city and the island do so and be allowed to make their escape by sea without threat."

"What else?"

"Those who stay in the city do not suffer any harm. We know what happened with other cities before. Truly, the Sicilian citizens did not take part in this action, and those who remain should not be punished. Nor should farmers and herders be subjected to any retribution, whose situation Roma should make every effort to improve."

"These are two. I assure you we can agree on terms for them to be met. I hope the third is not more difficult."

"It probably is. Though sympathy was hard to feel, I had extended mercy to some of those who had placed us in bondage. As you know, I released all the landowners appointed by Roma who did not commit crimes against people under their control. But neither mercy nor fairness was shown to Tiberius Gracchus, apparently a man of honour who was conspired upon and then murdered in Roma, for the mere reason that he wanted to enact fair agrarian laws to diminish the injustices against the farmers and improve the lot of the poor. Those with privilege who own many slaves and more land than they should made him the object of vicious attacks. So I ask you if you joined in the action against Gracchus."

"That I might have been part of the action is untrue. I stood aside in the quarrel," replied Rupilius haughtily, though with a hint of remorse. "I was asked later by the senate to join in an inquiry about the friends of Gracchus who posed a threat to public order. It was Publius Popillius Laenas who led the attacks."

"I heard a different account of your involvement. But even, you did not in effect raise your voice or lift a hand to stop this persecution, first of the man and later his supporters."

Rupilius looked aside for a moment, as if to evade the guilt, then turned to Younis and said somewhat harshly:

"This is not a matter of concern to you. There is nothing to be done about it now."

"The death of Gracchus dealt a blow to the rights of farmers and artisans. What he was trying to do has implications to what happens here in Sicilia with the landowners and slaves. Your landed aristocracy in the peninsula and here in Sicilia continued to exercise advantages over others, and used thousands of slaves throughout the countryside to work their huge estates and replace the small farmers. Endless supplies of more slaves replenished the ones whose strength had been leached and were considered disposable, like damaged raiment. That is the source of the unrest. It is not possible to stop rebellions without remedying the injustices in the system itself."

"We will do our best, but we cannot suddenly deprive the landlords of their properties and cause resentment and upheaval among them. These are our normal practices, choosing to place Roma above all, as is befitting. The gods witness our successes. As proconsul I have been commissioned to stay behind and organise the affairs of government on the island and introduce reforms. In those reforms, we are planning to consider the issues you raised. We need the farmers and herders," answered Rupilius, though Younis thought that such a promise was unlikely to be sufficiently fulfilled.

Rupilius stood up and continued, "You have your conditions. Tell me what preparations you will be making."

"We have arranged for ships to wait for us," replied Younis, as he stood also. "I will inform you when our columns move, in two or at most three days. We will take with us some landowners and other hostages, who will be released once my people are secure on board the ships."

"This is an unnecessary precaution, but I have no objection to it."

Younis had decided to take other precautions, though he felt almost sure that Rupilius would not engage in the usual treachery employed by other generals. He thought it wise to head first west as if toward Katane or Siracusai and then change direction to the south to reach the port of Gela with speed, where sixty ships to be paid for in gold were waiting to take them to various locations in the east.

"What we have agreed is unpleasant for both of us. You did not get your victory and we did not keep our dominion. We will be free elsewhere, and you will have Sicilia under your sway again. Many people have died in this fight, and there will be more deaths in future uprisings. As a man who honours his word, will you make the changes that give people more of their due rights?"

"We know what we are doing, what we must do."

"I doubt much good will come out of it otherwise. Neither one of us will live to see what happens in the distant future," said Younis, starting toward his men. Rupilius walked to his horse, donned his cloak and helmet, and rode off in the other direction.

Chapter 29

Satisfaction is hard to come by. It is never complete. Even as the ships approached their refuge destination in Arados, Younis kept thinking he must go to Afamia immediately to see his mother, and take Elissar, Dalia and 'Abdun with him. The demands of arrival in a new place had delayed this trip. Of the sixty ships that took the men, women and children from Gela, more than thirty-five headed first to Kypros and then to the Kilikian port of Tarsos. The remaining ships landed in Arados. From these two locations, the exiles were to spread out into towns and cities of their choosing. Kleon, who was still mourning his brother, was responsible for arranging dispersal from Kypros and Tarsos to other places. Younis and Elissar decided that the safest option was to stay in Arados, an island opposite Antarados and not far from Afamia, famous as a refuge. Its inhabitants were engaged mostly in trade and fishing, and it was somewhat independent of surrounding kingdoms, though not too many people could stay without drawing suspicion.

Upon reaching Afamia, they found out that his mother Maryam was gone. Neighbours told them she had passed more than three years before, so they searched and found her grave. They sat around the grave and shared a meal in her honour. They raised a blessing, speaking to her in hopes that she could hear and know they were close. What happiness it would have been for her to have seen them after an eternity of waiting and suffering, to have been alive with them, to have known her only son had returned, to love them and be loved by them, to hear Younis tell her that she was always on his mind in his every step.

Younis inquired about his old teacher Mani, as it seemed his obligation to do. Attendants at the school said he had stopped teaching a long time ago, and told him where to find his house. He held the door half open, bent over, his head now bald and his beard white and long. He did not recognise Younis at first, maybe because Elissar and the children were with him. He squinted, studying the smiles of his visitors searchingly, trying to remember. His dim eyes finally lit up with recognition. Perhaps it was the hair or the nose that brought the memory of a younger Younis to his mind. They embraced and cried. Younis did not ask Mani about his mother, he himself immediately told him that he had gone to tell her the evening of that day. "I informed her of what had happened, and tried to console her, to give her hope that your absence will not be long. I assured her that you will find a way to get back to her." It was a very special bond between mother and son in their situation, Mani realised, and had hoped that the land will call Younis back. He did not expect that his promise would be so strangely fulfilled. What happened eighteen years before had changed his life too, Mani confessed to them. For days after the event, he had been in pain and confusion, unable to accept the humiliation and helplessness of seeing five boys snatched from his care and delivered to the worst of worldly fates. "You are the first of the five boys or the others to return," he told them. To assuage his constant agony, of betraying the trust placed in him, he had decided to leave his profession. He no longer felt able to teach with confidence. As he spoke, he pointed to a pile of manuscripts as the product of the ensuing years. He said there were three books, the first about Zeno, a great philosopher who lived in Athênai though a native of this land. Another work he described dealt with gods and goddesses, as well as an account of religions now, and how several gods and goddesses in the pantheons had their origins in old regional mythology, which he had supported with conclusive evidence. Younis examined this book and thought it would be interesting to study it carefully later.

In an unexpected coincidence, Mani mentioned that he had almost finished a work about the ideal city and good government, his definition of what a ruler should do and how best to organise a society. These were subjects that others had written on before him, but he felt they should be supplemented with new perspectives. At this point, Younis was conflicted about how much to tell Mani about his own experiences. He resolved to say enough without getting into too much detail about the outcome or his present refuge. He informed Mani that after ten years in captivity, while at work tutoring two children, events in Enna escalated to such an intolerable degree. Repeated cruelties and executions committed by landowners and legionaries led to an uprising that circumstances obliged him to lead. Younis described what was wrong with Roma's system, its self-absorption and self-interest, especially as it applied to the lands of Sicilia. He depicted events and experiences leading up to the revolt, relating how he succeeded in bringing together not only slaves but also many farmers and herders who were equally oppressed and desirous of liberty. He mentioned some of the battles, the new laws they had tried to institute during the period, and how it all ensued. "Well," Mani responded, "I could see that side of your character before, so what you did is no surprise. How well did it succeed? Tell me more." Mani was keen to know even the smallest details, such as what improvements were introduced for farmers and crafts people, both those outside the city and those within.

"This is important," he said before they left him, "that you are here and that it happened. I am proud of you. It is unfortunate that it turned out that way and that Sicilia was forced back to its past condition. It is something to hold on to for the future. One happy result for certain is that you have found Elissar and that you brought children who are here for us to enjoy and see them grow. They are the future." As they shared more refreshments, Mani made Younis promise to return soon and bring Elissar, Dalia and 'Abdun with him.

Chapter 30

"Don't laugh too much, 'Abdun, your nose is not much smaller than mine." Sitting next to the coal burner giving some warmth in the cool autumn, 'Abdun had giggled when his father told them that during a recent trip to Afamia some people he knew in his youth recognised him most likely from his nose. It was a distraction this joking, the people having expressed their admiration for his endurance in a world turned inside out and overcoming a fate suffered by many.

"Yes, father, I'm proud of that. I'm proud of what you have done, and what mother has done. I remember a little of what it was like before we came here."

Dalia was stretching at the edge of the carpet, her head in Elissar's lap. "We have heard some of what happened before and after we were born. But tell us, father, why did events turn out the way they did? I often think about such things and can't understand everything about them." Perhaps Dalia's curiosity would be quenched by stories of adventure and exciting battles, or maybe she also sensed that there were questions and concerns she had missed.

"In past days, I told you some of what I had experienced after being caught by the king's men and shipped to Delos and then Sicilia. It was a tender age to be put into such distress, a bit older than you dear Dalia and 'Abdun and more than twice your age my little Hani. I was alone in more ways than one, something difficult for you to understand now that we are all together. Without a mother and father, family or friends, in bondage in a new place, my soul was in a state of loss and confusion. As the tutor of two children, a girl and a boy, I did all I could to pass on what knowledge I had and to get them to understand the world in a way different from what they knew in their own comfortable lives. I often wondered if it was possible for them to imagine how vast the world was and how other people thought and lived in other places and circumstances. But the meaning of that work was not enough to give me comfort or overcome my anxieties, so I tried to find solace in other tasks. The sharp contrast of my new life cut deeply into my youthful assumptions, and I could see more clearly the contradictions in the world that people have created. My soul cried out for an awareness I still had to discover. At first, I found meaning in seeing nature and everything else around me with new eyes and a different understanding, and I took to working with stones and rocks as a most natural calling, just as we have done here in the courtyard, by shaping structures and features out of them. It was as if by creating something special out of the silent stones I was telling my masters then that I was the one in control and not altogether a slave under their command. With these new images and feelings another world appeared I do not know how. It showed itself in a surety to foretell the future and in the feats of magic I started to perform. To be able to connect to a world different from the normal is not something easily explained. Only in a few people does such strangeness appear after they have suffered many trials and worries. It is as if what they pass through in fear and unease takes them beyond what is known into another sphere that others cannot imagine entering. Maybe you will understand it more when you are older. Years later, I met your mother. In each other we discovered more of ourselves and began to imagine another life we could build together. We gave each other certainty and purpose. We welcomed you into this life, dear ones, only after we broke the chains of slavery and could hope you would grow up free and proud. Maybe this answers some of your questions."

"Not really. You are telling us more about your personal experience, not what caused the events, what led to them," 'Abdun remarked probingly.

"How can I answer such a question in a simple way? One would have to go to the very beginning, the beginning of human experience that is, because what we had then, what we have now, is the result of one thing after another over a long period. Since time immemorial people have tried to find what some call meaning in life, why we are alive and think and behave the way we do, to explain what is difficult or impossible to explain about nature and existence. People wondered about the mysterious world that surrounded them and what meaning there could be in their daily lives, rife with uncertainty, unrest and fear. Of course, they must have rejoiced at the dawn of each sunrise and the renewal of life in spring, but whether they fully realised it or not, they also asked many questions in their desire to find direction, safety and certainty in the emptiness surrounding them. People even now still examine such questions, though they may have more comforts and pleasures. Imagine how immediate their puzzlement would have been in the earliest times. Why are we here? Who created the world we live in with such precision, and what formed the patterns of the stars and the sun and the moon? How do the birds know where to fly before winter sets in and when to return for spring? What brings the waters that grow our crops and the storms that destroy them? What comes after death? In those most ancient days, people still lived in nature and used as food what they could pick in wild berries and seeds and what they could hunt as meat and fish. Together they owned nature as a whole common to all of them. They were fewer people then but they found their answers to these questions from the nature in which they lived. Their answers were not all the same everywhere, but there was much similarity in the hopes and in the imagining."

"That sounds like a paradise," said Dalia playfully.

"Yes almost. It was a hard life, different from ours. Gradually, people changed. They made some animals obey them and planted seeds to harvest every year as food. They built villages and towns, and then cities and economies. They began trading and created notions of property and money. The gods and beliefs they derived from nature became fixed into gods and beliefs that served their own city or empire. Property they came to value as good for people to have for their own use, and for them to settle and shelter in one place. But with time when a few people saw they could prosper by collecting more property as their own, communities grew in uneven ways, as land and property increased in the hands of those few, which brought a change that started many evils. It is the same with money and riches. One piece of land was added to another and then another. That was how we got those who grew more powerful than others and called themselves lords, and under them those who survived by serving them, the multitude. Instead of having their share in the land that in the past was seen as the gift to all, most people became servants either by force or necessity and were left with little or nothing to own. Those lords together chose one whom they appointed as ruler or king, who then persuaded followers to believe his kingship was given by the gods, that he was the god's likeness on earth. As populations grew, to keep this system of power going and to revel in their might, the ones who ruled recruited armies to conquer more possessions, and in the process enslaved other people they defeated. Even when some states were formed into what were called republics, they were controlled by the same purpose of promoting self-interest and feeling superior to others. In the heat of such pursuits, greed grew to the point of blindness. Land is taken from others for the benefit of the few, animals are killed not only to feed one's own needs but to make profit, and gold and other metals deemed to be precious are dragged from the bowels of the earth to enrich the powerful. To justify their action, those in power invent the belief that they are better, nobler and more virtuous than those they conquer by arms or guile. The lure of such riches removes from their nature the idea that they could be happier just to have enough and to treat others as they would have others behave toward them. It becomes more profitable to gain advantage by exercising power over others than to build societies where people are equal."

"How does this explain what happened in Sicilia?"

"The fighting we had with our enemies resulted from this uneven history. Some humans still believed that by force of arms they could use others to their profit and deny them the right to freedom they inherited at birth. The oppressed cannot possibly continue to accept their oppression forever. They will eventually rise in rebellion to break their chains, as we did, when they realise that their oppressors do not really have more talents or abilities, that the gods those oppressors created in their own image and the methods used to justify their practices are neither true nor just. It is no wonder that in the old epic poems the forces struggle in never-ending opposition, light and darkness, order and disorder, good and evil, joy and pain, life and death. Unrest is a constant result. It is difficult to know how long the struggle would last, or what forms it might continue to take in the future. It is difficult to know if history will ever reflect a better, more just humanity than it has done until now.

"It is not all that easy to understand at once, I know. We must be careful not to simplify too much. But certainly those in power work to hide the truth of this history or even change it just enough to keep the people obedient. Their words spread because they have the tools to write, and they work to erase the writing of others and to keep people ignorant of their intentions. They make sure that only what they say stays in people's hands and minds. Empires sometimes try to mend their ways, making small improvements in order to last longer, but the high values they declare only hide the greed on which they are built. In the end nothing lessens the scourge of their power and the slavery that comes with it. When they wage wars for gain and control, they find excuses to make them seem just and righteous. Even their piracy is turned into good policy, cruelty into discipline, injustice made to appear as high and lawful principles."

"Why do they change the truth, pack events with lies, don't tell what really happened?" asked 'Abdun, reaching to the bowl for a small bunch of his favourites late-season black grapes they had just picked from the vine overhanging the courtyard.

"Their politicians and most of their historians make up rumours to protect their privilege. They want to show that those who complain have no good cause to do so, that it is useless to resist, and so leave people with the notion that rebels are doers of evil who cannot behave with heroism and nobility and deserve to be defeated. The powerful do not like anyone to question their own claim to profit. They want people to forget that rebellion comes because there is injustice, that it arises from the everlasting search for a place where the rules apply to everyone and all humans who breathe are the same. I have heard of stories that accuse us of wholesale murder of all men, women and even children, and of committing other heinous crimes. Such stories are spread to make us look cruel and ill-willed, and so deserving of condemnation. Of course, we did no such thing. I led a revolt to free enslaved people. We showed mercy even to those landlords who owned us, if they did not have blood on their hands. But we applied just laws to those who had murdered our people without reason, and meted out punishment in kind. One report says that at the end I escaped with a few hundred men into the mountains, and that my men killed each other by beheading to the last man. This is just another false report, foolish indeed but good for the gullible, circulated to make others think that dishonour and death is the inevitable end for those who resist. In another attempt to discredit us, it is said that I hid in a cave like a cowardly selfish man who would abandon his people to face retribution alone. As I also heard recently, my enemies still repeat the untruth that I was arrested and put in prison, though their writers contradict each other in their invention of where I was imprisoned. That should make anyone doubt everything else they say. Some also say that I died in this prison from a disease where my flesh was eaten up by a mass of lice coming from inside of me. Now my dears, try to imagine why they would invent such a disease?"

"I am wondering about that. Why?" asked Dalia.

"There were many others who were rumoured to have had the same death, as I read in books. In all cases they were people who had enemies who disliked them or disagreed with their beliefs or opinions, or thought of them as competitors, or envied their talents. Such rumours lodge in the imagination. It becomes easy to assume that ones who die from this affliction have been cursed by the gods and so deserve to suffer. The horror of this death is not to be feared as much as its dreadful falseness. The only lice that bit me are the lice that bite everyone else in their beds as they sleep. The legions of Roma did not catch me or put me in prison, nor did they hang me to die on a piece of wood as they have done to others. Their purpose in spreading such rumours is to ruin the fame of a people's resistance and make those who are still oppressed believe that anyone who comes to lead them will meet a terrible end. They want to weaken trust among those who are enslaved and hope to make it impossible for them to succeed.

"Now I will tell you the truth of what happened as facts you should keep. Our just revolt was a spark that started uprisings in many other places, and now I hear more are still happening, and will go on happening. We were able to defeat the armies sent against us, many times over for almost eight years. We made new law for all the people in one island on this earth. The empire continued to send more and more legions intent on destroying our threat to it by force and treachery. It could not tolerate a comparison between its rule and our dominion. Finally, it sent a huge army, and encircled our capital. I could have remained in Enna and kept it as a small fortress of freedom for many years. But how can freedom survive for long if so confined? The commander of Roma's legions, who camped outside the walls, could not take the city and wanted an agreement. After the long siege, I decided I did not want to be responsible for the death of more among those who believed in our cause. He was keen to avoid a repetition of the humiliation Roma's earlier armies had suffered at our hands. It was agreed to let our people take the ships that brought us to these shores. I made him promise not to harm the citizens in Enna, or the herders and farmers who stayed, not to repeat the punishments inflicted on other cities by the commanders of Roma. At least, by coming here and saving many people, we succeeded in breaking the oppression though we did not remove it altogether."

"So what are we supposed to do in the future?" asked ʿAbdun, sounding a bit restless.

"It is about how much we can learn from the past and how to tell it, to protect the gains we have made. I hope the stories I gave you will remain in your thoughts, that you will remember them well and give them to your children and grandchildren. Other things will happen that you must write as well and make known to others so they understand. It is necessary for us to write down our history by ourselves and know how to keep our own books alive. If we do not, our history will disappear or only others will write it for us to read. You already study many subjects in school and what you read you have to examine for the truth, wherever the truth may be. Though that is not always clear to see, you must try to discover why the truth is not always told, why so often it is hidden, why it must constantly be protected.

"Above all we must be alert to the designs of those who have ambitions to win control over us, who often try to sow divisions among us and make us fight each other, or to help them against our own. This is what Roma did to our country. After the death of the great Antiokhos, who was forced to make a treaty with Roma, the senate in Roma made sure to support one claimant to the throne against another, which led to battles and death, and made the king-dom only weaker with time. That's what Roma's senate also did with Qart Ḥadašt, encouraging a neighbour kingdom, Numidia, to fight against it, a neighbour who should have respected the bonds of blood and culture between them instead. Roma used this as an excuse to attack Qart Ḥadašt and with Numidia's help destroyed it. What did Numidia gain? In the short term maybe some spoils, but it only became a servant of Roma, and was later itself conquered and turned into a province under Roma's rule. I wonder what we learn from all that."

"We should work together and know the common enemy," ʿAbdun answered right away.

"Yes, it is good that you say it that way. Otherwise, we remain divided and weak. Often I ask myself how much people have learned from the past. More than what I have done, what all the brave men and women risked together with me is worthy of remembrance. I hope it will influence what others do in the future. Will slavery in all its shapes and forms disappear? Can we hope for that if we remain blind to the dishonesty and injustice on which its practices are built? Will greed be made a crime to be exposed rather than the power that rules? Does the future hold goodness or more conflict? I ask these questions because they matter more than my story alone. I myself wonder if I have done enough, and whether I could have done some things differently."

"We cannot repair the past and what it brought in sadness. But we can look ahead to the future," Elissar said after her long silence. "I told you what happened in Qart Ḥadašt, in my country, and all the destruction carried out by power and greed. It stays with me all the time like a bad dream. I lost my mother and my father, your grandmother and grandfather, and all the people I knew there. Still, I hold the hope that the same destruction will not be allowed to happen like a ritual again to anyone anywhere. The past cannot but find ways of showing it is not fulfilled, and truth must reach out from the darkness of ignorance and deceit. Without the light of truth, we cannot find a saving grace and the right future. We have comfort in the fact that some people were saved from the weight of oppression, and we know there will be more in times to come. You remember Fadi and Lamia. You visited with their children last year. Fadi now uses his first name as a free man after keeping the name Nilos for a long time. Fadi has a large farm in a town called Manbij and Lamia helps in teaching the children. You met Mikhaila, who found her life's mate here. You played with her children, Hani. We are so happy to have such proud spirits living among us. These are only a few out of the thousands who are now free and will stand for the freedom of others, no matter where they live. In you and in them we keep the thoughts and cherish the dreams. Though they, as we, have gained freedom, filling with wind many sails, many people are still suffering. It is up to us, and you, not to forget and to keep the hope alive that truth and freedom will win in the end."

The ears of the drowsy children pricked up with Elissar's words. "You should know and be careful about what you read and hear, that's what your father is saying," Elissar continued. "You must do so because most of the time we do not have the other side of history, of those who have been abused, certainly not our side most of the time. You must do so because some of those who write and record often have a purpose to serve, and continue to change the facts and to create fictions. You must study more, question, think and think more on everything you can find. Your father has accomplished much, although he likes to say he has not done enough. You must continue to hold his banner high. More than anything else, you must work to foil the designs of those who only wish to benefit themselves at your expense and who do not work for the good of everyone alive but only their own. Make sure that their trickery does not work and that past mistakes are not repeated by us, as human beings are liable to do in their weakness. Make sure, my beloved, to tell the people now and later not to allow others to sow division in order to rule them more easily and rob them of the rights they deserve."

It was a long time talking this evening, longer than they ever did before. "You are getting sleepy I see and need to rest, dears. You can ask us questions later if you want to know more," Younis said to the children. "Come now, embrace me. Go to your mother and kiss her and wish her a morning of wellness."

Epilogue

Sicilia and Syria
2010

I t's been a long way coming to Enna to stand at last before this statue. Am I here where both of us have walked? What had moved me to search out the seldom examined history of the man commemorated here and events of his life more than two thousand one hundred years after his passing?

Larger than life, the bronze statue depicts a muscular youth standing atop a mound sprouting vines and weeds. Behind it lies the striated rock on which rise the walls of a fortress now called Lombardy Castle. The young man has an exaggerated chest that tapers to a slender waist, a body naked except for a slight loincloth, and neatly stylised cornrows on the head. The right arm is raised high, grasping a large chain which has been broken in half, while the lowered left hand holds the other half of the chain that had held him in bondage. His hairless face is contorted by a mouth that's open wide in a fateful cry of freedom that he and those with him had longed for in a strange land where he was forced to lead the genesis of change. Here he is: a memorial and a contradiction. What made him who he was to become?

I cross to the edge of the escarpment toward a dark green cypress and scan the hills below. No wonder this natural fortress was almost impossible for ancient armies burdened with weapons to breach except by repeated acts of trickery. It lies on a large plateau perched on top of a gigantic hill—almost a mountain—surrounded by precipitous cliffs. Established by local Sicani more than 3000 years ago, it has over centuries been repeatedly overcome, like the rest of Sicily, by many conquerors: Greeks, Carthaginians, Romans, Byzantines, Muslims, Normans, and others, leaving behind

Statue of "Euno" in Enna
(Wikimedia Commons)

remnants of their own buildings, beliefs and habits. The conquerors have moved on or been integrated into the native population, but Enna remains where it has always been, atop the heights. The highest inhabited location in Italy at 931 metres, it is literally the island's centre—umbilicus Siciliae, the navel of Sicily. And the right home for the man they called Eunus or Euno, Younis, and for his destined revolt.

I walk back to the statue and touch it, and look toward the rock wall where a white marble plaque reads, in translation: "Two thousand years before Abraham Lincoln liberated the Black peoples, the humble slave Euno courageously sent out the cry of freedom from this Sicilian fortress to his companions in ill fortune, and affirmed the right of every human being to be born free and to die free. In remembrance of the significance of this act, the municipality of Enna has placed this memorial in the year 1960."

View of Enna

A bridge in Enna I just passed is called Ponte Euno. The plaque seems intended to appeal to tourists, though it's uncertain how the comparison between Lincoln and "Euno" would actually work, unless generous imagination steps in. It reminds me somewhat of the ambivalent Statue of Freedom that crowns the dome of the U.S. Capitol. The plaque does not inform us who those "companions" were or against whom they fought for freedom. It's also not clear how this commemoration of the past relates to a system in the present that affiliates with those who enslaved "Euno" and his companions. The statue doesn't look like anything I could draw from my readings about the man or the coinage that bears his likeness. Nor was he the kind of slave who was kept in chains.

A coincidence had led me onto this journey to places like Sicily and Syria that didn't occupy my interest before, to begin the search to recreate this ancient revolt. It all started when I was taking a graduate course on slavery in Greece and Rome at the School of Classics. A long reading list included historical readings from Herodotus, Thucydides, Xenophon, Polybius, Cato, Diodorus, Livy, Strabo, Plutarch, Florus, Appian, Tacitus, Orosius, and others, as well as works by philosophers and other writers like Aristotle, Zeno, Plautus and Petronius, Varro and Columella. As background, the course outline included a one-week overview of works from earlier periods in the ancient world, including ancient Eygpt, Mesopotamia and the Bible. For my research paper I had picked Diodorus Siculus, for no reason at first except that the name struck me as having a special ring to it. Diodorus wrote a world history in forty books, some of which have survived completely, while fragments of the lost books were preserved by later historians. He was born in Agira a few decades after the "Euno" revolt. Serendipity! Agira, I now discover, is a short drive from where the statue stands.

I located Diodorus' account of a slave revolt in Sicily between about 140 and 132 BCE, which though fairly short is still the most extensive description available. I read some related articles and books by classicists and modern historians. Wow, I thought, this topic is endless, with all sorts of digressions into history, philosophy, literature, law, politics, warfare, even psychology and demonology, and comparative slavery across the ages. I didn't grasp at first how much these readings would lead to yet more connections—and questions about what I used to accept about the records, gaps and cautions of human history. Above all, I couldn't possibly guess then how much this research would alter the course of my life.

Diodorus tells us that the revolt was led by a "Syrian" named "Eunus," an entertainer and magus belonging to Antigenes of Enna. The slaves of a particularly cruel landowner, Damophilos, approached "Eunus" to ask whether the gods would favour their uprising. The timing was opportune and answered to the aspirations of the few hundred slaves who took over Enna under his leadership. Their number grew to hundreds of thousands across the island, as the movement attracted not only slaves but also disgruntled shepherds and farmers whose work and energies held no interest for the privileged except the profit they gained from them. "Eunus" defeated several Roman armies. For the people, these victories were a clear trumpeting of the gods' attentive favour, and so "Eunus" was able to establish himself as "king." Diodorus does not mention anything about his leadership skills in bringing together disparate groups or his state-building activities, though there's an indication of that in the minting of coins, a few now kept in museums in Siracusa and London or by collectors.

"Eunus" coin, c. 135 BCE
(Museo Archeologico Regionale "Paolo Orsi", Siracusa)

Diodorus identifies the rebellious elements as "Syrian," probably as a reflection of conflict with the Seleucids or some other biases. It is difficult to believe that all of them came from Syria as it's now called. Most likely some were survivors from Carthage after its destruction in the final "Punic war," so in this sense "Syrian" too. Surely others were captives from other Roman conquests in Greece, the Iberian Peninsula, and various places across the Mediterranean. Being a Sicilian of Greek background living under Roman rule, Diodorus may have wanted to distance Hellenes and Sicilians from what happened by ascribing the revolt to Syrians only, despite evidence that the insurrection appealed to disadvantaged Sicilians and to Hellenistic culture.

Diodorus enumerates atrocities committed by the self-freed slaves: women raped, masters slaughtered, even "suckling babes they tore from the breast and dashed to the ground." Under siege in one city, the rebels are described as monsters that ate children and women, and later "did not abstain even from eating one another." Not only were they merciless murderers and child killers, we are led to believe, but cannibals as well. One inconsistency occurs in a brief reference to the rebels allowing some Roman dependents to leave unharmed under escort. Though Diodorus alludes to mal-treatment as a motivation for the atrocities, there's no way to find out what else happened or what else would supplement or con-tradict these reports. All extant accounts sound much like old and more recent histories that demonise those who resist invasion or oppression, labeling them as savages and cannibals, pagans and beasts, vagabonds and terrorists, incapable of civilised behaviour. The powerful, comfortable in a life of privilege and oppression of others, can readily employ strategies to guard their interests and fabricate accounts to preserve the status quo won by force with-out forfeiting their advantage. In such cases, it becomes difficult to separate facts from tropes.

I grew more skeptical as I read descriptions of how the revolt ended. In a city besieged by the Romans, the rebels were betrayed by another "Syrian," a typical strategy to raise suspicion and sow division. "Eunus" is depicted as a selfish fraudster who abandons his followers, contrary to what one would expect from his earlier actions. As Roman legions besieged Enna, "Eunus" is reported to have fled with a thousand men to a mountainous region, where the thousand, fearing their fate, killed each other by beheading. It is further said that "Eunus," in cowardice, hid in a cave with his cook, baker, masseur and entertainer. According to Diodorus, he was dragged out of the cave and remanded in Morgantina where his flesh was consumed by a mass of lice. Plutarch says that "Eunus" was taken to Rome after his capture, where he died of this same disease that infected Sulla. Another source mentions Siracusa as his place of imprisonment. Why are the prison locations different in various accounts? Why didn't those one thousand rebels fight to the end instead of beheading each other? Why didn't "Eunus" receive the usual swift public execution?

And what about this ugly death he is said to have suffered? Otherwise called phthiriasis or morbus pedicularis, the disease has been characterized in ancient and more recent times as the fate of those unapproved of in official history for political or religious reasons, or otherwise suspected or disliked. There's a long list of those reported to have been afflicted with this disease, including Akastus son of Pelias (enemy of Achilles' father), Queen Pheretima of Cyrenaica and King Xerxes of Persia (in Herodotus), Socrates, even Plato and his nephew Speusippos (rumoured by enemies of the Academy), the Spartan poet Alkman and Syrian-born philosopher Pherecydes (as reported by Aristotle and others), the historian Kalisthenes (placed in fetters by Alexander the Great), arguably the Egyptians plagued by lice in Exodus, Quintus Pleminius (disgraced Roman propraeter), Antiochos IV Epiphanes (allied with Hellenised Jews but considered the "wicked one" in traditionalist rabbinical sources), Mucius the jurist and Lucius Sulla who revived the dictatorship (as reported by Plutarch), Quintus Pleminius the legate of Scipio Africanus (who desecrated the temple of Proserpina), Herod the Great (one of multiple symptoms, according to Flavius Josephus, employing the literary topos for a tyrant's death, borrowed later by Eusebius), Herod Agrippa (in Acts 12:23), Gaius Galerius and Valerius Maximianus (who persecuted early Christians), Julius Julianus (as per Philostorgius, who attributes this fate to the uncle and supporter of Julian "the Apostate," the last Byzantine emperor to reinstate paganism, who couldn't have been similarly afflicted having obviously died young in a battle with the Persians), the Vandal king Huneric (who exiled Christian bishops), Arnulf of Carinthia (disputed king of Italy and the Holy Roman Empire), Elfhere ealdorman of the Mercians (enemy to monks, accused of involvement in the murder of King Edward the Martyr), King of Leinster Diarmait Mac Murchada (who profaned and burned Saints of Ireland churches and was accused of having brought the English to regain his kingdom), Ivan the Terrible of Russia, John Calvin (according to some clergymen), Philip II of Spain and Portugal, Swedish Archbishop Abraham Angermannus, Parliamentary leader John Pym (supporters of Charles I, insisting that he had perished from "the foul disease of Herod" by divine punishment despite contrary evidence, disinterred and then despoiled his body after the Restoration), and many other instances. Is such a disease, selectively applied, like cannibalism, another hateful trope designed in this case to vilify rebel leaders beyond redemption and discourage future uprisings? Such questions urged me even more to search for ways to discover an alternative narrative, despite the formidable challenge of finding reliable and unbiased sources.

About two weeks before the end of semester, there was a bit of an unexpected altercation during discussion in class, which puzzled me when it grew into somewhat tense exchanges. I would normally go to the library after class and then to the apartment for dinner. Instead, I decided to find a place to relax and try to grasp what had just happened. I also felt the pressure to finalise the paper and fine-tune the introduction. I took a side street to a little run-down dinette, which I like because most times it was not busy and the friendly owner, Alvita, knew the magic of creating a fragrant welcome for a passer-by. I sat at my favourite table in the corner, exchanged pleasantries and asked about Alvita's small daughter who had been at her grandmother's home with a fever. With coffee and cake, I started to draft the introduction.

My intention was to highlight the implications of this event as one of the early great slave revolts in history, unique in its characteristics, and to analyze biases in its presentation in ancient and modern sources. Some classicists today argue that rebel leaders in that period didn't really have a political consciousness, nor did they possess a clear idea of what they wanted to achieve by their actions, that their purpose was to rule in the same way, replacing their oppressors only with different hands. It is as if to love freedom is a new invention, except when it suits us to think otherwise as a reflection of our own ideology or when it pertains to figures we favour. In the case of Leonidas, several hundred years before "Eunus," the usual narrative leaves no doubt about the heroism and the fight for higher values and for liberty. Especially in the film, it is made to seem that only 300 courageous Spartans stood against the multitude of invading Persians, when in fact Leonidas' army included thousands of citizens from other Greek cities and also helots, essentially Spartan slaves or serfs promised freedom if they fought. In the big screen portrayal, the Persians are made into absolute evil, reflecting it appears current animosities toward Iran. Wouldn't the exploits of Aristomenes of Messinia against Spartan domination, or Aristonikos of Pergamon against the urban rich and Roman expansion, be more relevant to the struggle for freedom?

Spartacus is an admirable figure of course. He has been glamorised into an icon in novels, plays, musical compositions, films and TV series. He has grown into a myth, an axial figure, first by anti-tyranny movements in France, then for other reasons in post-unification Italy and in the Soviet Union. He has become a liberty bell, a Marxist or socialist precursor, even a kind of Christ, or a commentary on slavery in America. In Koestler's *Gladiators* the story represents the failure of Utopia. The story of Spartacus was touted but also feared. Hoover himself intervened to prevent publishers from accepting Howard Fast's Spartacus novel. Why do people promote and embellish only selected stories, such as that of the fictional Ben-Hur? Spartacus tried to cross to Sicily to save his uprising, to escape being cornered, and to find a more defensible geography. Did the Thrace-born gladiator perhaps know of what "Eunus" had done six decades before? What about other far-reaching, long-lasting rebellions against enslavement and tyranny, before and after? Only recently are more of the insurrections against slavery in the Americas beginning to be brought out into public awareness and recognised as legitimate human reactions. "Eunus" led a great uprising by slaves and the poor, and sustained it over an extended period, certainly longer than Spartacus'. It was followed by two similar revolts in Sicily by Salvius and Athenion. Are there reasons that prevent these other major events from being more equally recognised?

As a partial explanation for this selective recognition, I wrote into the introduction what I had mentioned during class discussion about the construct of Western civilization. I had referenced a book and two articles that trace its development, and mentioned a few scholars who have made it possible to advance new perspectives. One source points out that only since the sixteenth century has this construct developed as an operative system in the way we know it and accept it today. It's a convenient triple amalgam of select elements from Greek culture, Roman precedents, and serviceable biblical notions. The emergence of this adopted construct coincided with the rise of colonization in the Americas and across the globe, and it proved to be helpful in implementing imperialistic policies and promoting self-interest by various powers. These elements often contradict each other but are sanitised to reconcile inconsistencies among them and contradictions between espoused principles and real practices. In the process of owning a peculiar sense of identity by appropriating such elements, the construct elides influences from earlier civilizations. It conceives of Greek culture as a "miracle" of origins that supply philosophical depth and the beginnings of democracy, while often forgetting the formative influences of Egyptian and, even less acknowledged, Cana'anite civilizations on Greece, something the ancient Greeks themselves did not deny. Is eliding the Cana'anites (called "Phoenicians" by the Greeks, a term now sometimes used euphemistically) perhaps the result of their being demonised in biblical narratives? It proves useful as well to adopt Roman models in such aspects as laws, war, treaties and architecture, admiringly, despite Rome's destruction of other civilizations (like the Etruscan, which it nevertheless appropriated), and its nefarious empire-building practices. For the construct to supply religious validity, it incorporates the Bible as a justifying belief system, employing concepts such as a racial "chosen people" and a specially constructed god who favours them, and adopting narratives to validate various colonial projects: the conquest of the New World as the "Conquest of Canaan" and its native people cursed as idolatrous Cana'anites or Philistines who deserve to be dispossessed and exterminated. I was tempted to add, though I decided it was as such not directly relevant to my topic, that the biblical narratives people assume to be historical have been questioned by archaeological and scholarly findings, with many of them shown to be adaptations from earlier mythological antecedents and stories by other people. More germane, the biblical god worshipped as the one and only, Yahweh, has been shown to be one god in a pantheon headed by the chief father god El, as even shown in the text of Deuteronomy 32: 8-9 from the Dead Sea Scrolls discovery—a startling polytheism, from as late as the first century BCE, edited out by scribes who changed words to hide it in the later Masoretic version people still read today.

I was working with these ideas when the waitress, who gives her name as Lizzie (though I heard Alvita call her by another name), told me they are preparing to close. It was too late for the bus, so I began the long walk to my apartment, finding my thoughts back in the classroom.

My friend Janet, a doctoral student in history, told me after class, "Well, Maddie, this was threatening for some, though I liked some of what you said." I answered that I didn't mind it being so, "I thought our going to university included the purpose of debating such issues." I was recalling other arguments in class that I needed to incorporate into the introduction, especially how the construct implements biases. Why should we continue to accept selected historical and other texts as reliable classical precedents without serious scrutiny or reservation? Why don't we notice the gaps and inconsistencies, the biased descriptions of people and events, as much as we should? Is our partial blindness the result of our desire to identify with these texts, to believe them and hold them close as part of ourselves, to own them as tradition and heritage?

"There is much to admire about the Hellenes and even the Romans, but there's also excessive over-admiration," I remember saying. "Shouldn't we appreciate as much, or some would say more, the earlier civilizations of Egypt, Mesopotamia, Canaʻan, Assyria and other cultures whose formative accomplishments spread across the Mediterranean basin and were adopted by the Hellenes, by the Romans and others, and by us—inventions, ideas, religions, architecture, sciences, literature, and don't forget the Canaʻanite alphabet we all use until now. Without Egypt and Canaʻan there would have been no 'Greek miracle,' no birthing of democracy as it's called. Without the earlier regional mythologies, there would have been no creation myth or flood story in the Bible, as we now discover from the Epic of Gilgameš and other inscriptions and seals. There are many inconsistencies in this construct of civilization we have created. We really must recognise and study the precedents, understand the roots of our beliefs and assumptions, rather than feel threatened by what could be revealed about our assumed truths. Unfortunately, the few scholars who are striving to reinstate recognition of earlier influences and the significance of discoveries are often attacked by the classical and religious establishments."

A classmate, Jim, who had long hair and was writing a dissertation on eighteenth-century literature, questioned me about what I called inconsistencies in the construct, and added that he had the impression that I didn't give much credit to the advances made by the West. I was prepared for that kind of challenge and so answered immediately: "I'm not at all trying to discredit the accomplishments of any civilization or religious ideology, but rather to complete the picture. Why are the Romans presented as the oppressors in Philistia in the story of Christ at the same time that their laws, their structures, their treaties, obviously their architecture, have been adopted as precedents for imperial powers in the West? Many public buildings in Washington, D.C. are neo-Roman. And look at the ways people declare adherence to the New Testament message of love and forgiveness, a laudable message but hardly ever applied in practice. The story of Christ contains very fundamental aspects that are a continuation of much earlier regional mythology, but we see its elements of virgin birth, son of God and resurrection as uniquely miraculous. In the colonization of America, it was the Old Testament that provided the operative justifications for conquest, dispossession and genocide, with religious leaders and settlers identifying the native people of the Americas with the idolatrous enemies of ancient Israelites in biblical stories. This condemnation of idolatry doesn't affect the admiration showered on ancient Greek or Roman polytheism and its many gods, who are integrated in artistic expression and in linguistic and literary allusions. Why should we accept to view the Cana'anites as worthless idolaters or mere profiteering traders when they developed a polytheistic mythology that was partly copied in Greece and in fact also resulted in what is called monotheism? Isn't it ironic that, as we find out, the god used to condemn idolatry in the Bible is one in a pantheon of gods developed by the very people condemned as idolators? Why should the images of Babylonians, Philistines or Assyrians be seen through a biblical lens, or the Carthaginians through the Punic enmities of Rome? It seems we are far too invested in the construct to leave it."

Some classmates seemed startled by what I was saying. I was surprised the professor allowed the argument to go on. After a short uneasy quiet, my classmate Karen remarked:

"I agree that institutional investments, architecture and civic and religious structures are geared in that direction. Granted that most scholarship privileges the construct, and many careers are built on it, but don't you think it gives people some order and historical continuity. Questioning the foundational system too much affects our very identity. Who else can hold and protect the progress we have already built? We uphold the best traditions in good faith, and use the heritage we have adopted to benefit ourselves and also others. We protect the antiquities safe in museums so others can see what has been bequeathed from the past. Most people, even if they hear what you're saying, wouldn't see the logic in giving up the purpose and direction all these traditions still give us in our ongoing search for human development. What kind of benefit would come from losing the ability we have to influence events and ideas?"

"Perhaps we should. Perhaps losing some power and privilege would be better for us, would make us strong in fact, less afraid to see, not to mention that it would be better for others," I answered, being reminded by Karen's comments of where and how most museums acquired their ancient collections.

Now "Euno" urged me on.

"What bothers me more in what I read is that selective admiration for these three elements continues to demonise the oppressed people who rebel, or whose writings have not survived to give their perspective, but also forgets glaring examples of brutal practices by the oppressors. Only certain heroes are extolled, and others not. There are of course many aspects to be admired about what Rome accomplished in its development. At the same time, the Romans made it routine practice to massacre unarmed civilians and enslave people to benefit the empire and to profit themselves. They thanked their gods and offered sacrifices for their success. Their wars were always assigned a casus belli, whether against those they called barbarians or others who were civilised competitors to be eliminated, invoking the gods to sanction their actions. Like other imperial powers before and after them, they constructed a pyramid of excuses, topped by divine instruction and assistance to justify unquenchable nefariousness and greed, constructing a history (as still happens) for the purpose of buttressing ideologies of imperial expansion and subjugation of others thought to be inferior. It's a convenient system of power and self-interest, duplicitous and far too materially rewarding not to continue to be followed."

"I didn't know about these massacres, except in Carthage, which was the result of war. What about other examples?" Jim inquired.

"Yes, war with a hateful excuse that was fabricated, making it appear as if it broke the old treaty, so as to destroy the newly thriving Carthage as a commercial competitor. Korinth was destroyed in the same year with similar motives and results. Elsewhere look at Livy's account of how a Roman commander exterminated the whole population of a city, all unarmed civilians, to teach others a lesson in allegiance. One such massacre occurred in Enna, decades before the revolt I'm studying. The people were tricked to make them assemble in one place so the killing would be complete. Such massacres were repeated in Sicily, in the Iberian Peninsula and other places. Livy is not sure whether such crimes were heinous or justified as necessary for the project of empire. Shouldn't this remind us of similar atrocities in more recent centuries committed here among us? Or take other accounts I'm reading, which don't make sense except as a strategy to validate imperial rule and dissuade people from resistance. They read like cautionary tales meant to instruct rich slave owners to remain wary and slaves to distrust leaders of resistance. What historians have left for us to read demonises rebels and represents their leaders as dishonest and self-serving, as cowards, as cannibals. Doesn't that remind you of what happened in the Americas and around the globe during colonization, and before and after? Diodorus describes this leader of the Sicilian revolt as someone who, in the end, abandons his people and wants to gain the luxuries of masters for himself, and says about him: 'He claimed to foretell the future, and deceived many.' Why should he be assumed to have deceived people? What was the deceit? Which side is deceitful?"

Jim looked at the book, which was open to the page where I was reading, and asked after a moment: "Maybe he did deceive them. How could anyone foretell the future and do all these magical acts mentioned here?"

I wasn't intending to get into religion, since I knew Jim to be somewhat inclined that way. "So you think it's acceptable for people to believe in all those other incredible miracles as true. If you accept those wonders, isn't it possible for this person who came from that part of the world to have possessed some of the same powers? And what is prophecy anyway? Aren't people sometimes put into a situation where foretelling the future, or connecting to another world, grows out of their predicament?"

"I'm not sure I understand. Not all of us believe the miracles to be literally true."

"But you still privilege one book as special and holy although some of its accounts were copied from earlier mythologies. Shouldn't we enlarge the definition of what is holy? Even if such miracles are not believable, the metaphysical power of a few to see possibilities for a different future may be part of human nature, instilled by a longing for betterment and justice."

I went away from that class meeting with the impression that there was some anxiety that if we were to pursue a critical line of thinking too much we might end up with more uncertainty about our system. While I understood that inherited traditions held an enduring appeal, I had hoped that such discussion would lead to alternative considerations.

In the coming weeks, as I completed the paper (I found out later that the professor gave me an A in the course, though I had feared demotion) I kept thinking *I have to leave.* I didn't tell family and friends about my plans at first. I applied for a passport, booked a ticket, and sent for my visas. I was to travel in early February, with a late summer return date. I would miss the second semester for sure, if not more.

By going to Enna and to the ruins of Afamia, some connections could perhaps be recovered even now. Or the landscape would speak to me and take me back in time to what may have happened. (I experienced some incredible coincidences there, strange and unforeseen, and what they told me influenced my beliefs.) How could what I write be by necessity not just conjecture, not only historical fiction, but a more fully realised history? How can I use the sources but not necessarily follow them?

To start, I tried to settle the question about the name "Eunus" or "Euno." Using a clue incidentally mentioned by Diodorus that the name contains "a favourable omen that suggested good will toward his subjects," it was only possible to conclude that "Eunus" is a Greek form of the fairly common name Younis, which fits the meaning and the place of his birth. Nothing is told in any historical version about how he fell into bondage, where, when and why. What made him the one who speaks, persuades and acts? What events and signals triggered the people's revolt? How did Younis succeed in bringing together so many segments of the population, not only "Syrian" slaves but slaves from other regions and also farmers, shepherds and the poor across the island? What convictions did he hold for what state to create, his ideals for a future once he wrested Sicily from Roman hands? How did the revolt relate to what happened before it, especially the destruction of Carthage less than a decade earlier? The woman who became his queen— who was she and what was her role? What about the other nameless women rendered invisible in the historical accounts, perhaps out of fear that such inclusivity would humanise the rebellion? Though some may argue that women did not have a significant role in such events during that period, weren't they subjected to the same injustices against which the men revolted? Who supported the men, held the home base, kept families together, prepared the food, cared for the wounded, and helped in making weapons? We know there were women fighters in those times, and likely some would have joined the men in battle. How did Younis succeed in winning so many battles against the Roman legions? What can we envisage about an undescribed play mentioned by Diodorus that the rebels performed outside the walls of a besieged city? To what extent should we believe historical accounts about how this insurrection ended?

Florus writes in *Epitome of Roman History*, half deferentially, after listing the defeated Roman commanders Hypsaeus, Manlius, Lentulus, and Piso, that "the seriousness of our defeats causes his name to be remembered." I decided to write the kind of history that remembers his name as well as it should and fills in the missing spaces—a history that would give the people voice to speak and raise their memory across the time that separates and joins us.

As the loneliness of my writing neared its end, I was still overwhelmed by a sense of incompleteness. *Is there anything I have missed?* I decided to make another journey to Syria and to Afamia.

On the bus from Ḥamā, I was lucky to get the first seat to the right of the driver, which is more comfortable and has the best view of the countryside. The ticket collector, who acts as a kind of host, was busy going back and forth in the aisle offering coffee, a thermos in one hand and paper demitasses in the other. When he returned to the front, I struck up a conversation with him and the driver to practice my Arabic.

I had started to learn Arabic using a textbook and tapes while still at university, and then took classes in Dimaŝq for two months during my first visit. My interest in Arabic has somewhat different motives from those of most people. I don't see it only as a world language, or as one in which the Qu'ran was written, or as helpful for business, spying on locals, or other practical uses. I don't see it merely as a language associated with the people of what was given the colonial appellation "Middle East," and all the interventions and the troubles that have been brewing ever since Western powers carved up the region into spheres of influence or mandates. Some of its native speakers have themselves been taught to truncate their history with more recently acquired identities, sometimes a destructive self-colonising mindset. Many in the West have been taught to think of Arabic in more limited ways, or don't appreciate enough its richness and depth, its history long before Islam, or the pioneering works in science, medicine and philosophy that were written using the language when Europe was still in the Dark Ages, or the continuities that have made it the live storehouse of more ancient languages and dialects, or its calligraphic beauties. Recent political developments have only increased misperceptions. It's sad what has befallen a region from which others have so generously borrowed, often hiding that borrowing to camouflage the appropriated cultural heritage. Why not acknowledge and celebrate these civilizations that made the earliest achievements in human progress, in domestication of wildlife and in settlement, in city-building and architecture, in creating the first great epic, in inventing writing systems and especially the Cana'anite alphabet that has enabled us to put a small number of simple letters together to form the words we read with ease today? For the most part, I was studying Arabic in the hope that it would open another window onto the world and connect to my story and its roots in the distant past.

"How far is it to Afamia?" I attempted.

"About one hour and a half, insha-allāh," answered the ticket man, obviously pleased I was trying to speak in Arabic.

"You are going to see the ruins," inquired the driver. I didn't understand the last word, so I asked what "athār" means. He explained that it is what remains of the past, the "Roman" columns and temples. People often refer to ruins as "Roman" as if they had nothing to do with them, as if nothing came before the Romans, even when the ruins are not Roman.

"Yes. I am also looking for some information from the past," I ventured as if I expected help.

"What are you looking for?"

"I am searching for something that happened more than two thousand years ago in Afamia, anything that remains about a person who lived there."

"We are all remnants of the past," the driver retorted, laughing, relishing his own humour.

I decided to be more specific, having committed myself to the subject, though it was somewhat naïve to hope for anything to come of it.

"There was a man born in Afamia at a time long past. His name was Younis. He was taken as a slave to Siqilya and is known in history for a revolt against the Romans. I want to see if it's possible to find any trace, anything about him."

"Younis! Half the people in Afamia belong to the Younis family."

"Really?" I didn't know how to answer.

This was puzzling. Was it coincidence that this name, which I had assumed to be a forename, which I hear used today, is the title for an extended family, a *hamuleh*, of all the strangest places here in his home town? It is customary for an ancestor's first name to be used as a family name in this part of the world, but one from so ancient a time is still unusual. Perhaps Younis had used his patronym. A name to have survived more than two thousand years seemed miraculous or impossible. The past lingers in a multitude of peculiar ways. I decided to ask about this upon reaching the village.

Even before going up the hill to see the columns and temples of the ancient city, I inquired at a shopkeeper's. He indicated that I should go see the village mayor, ʿAbdulkarim Younis. "Is it possible to visit him now?" "Certainly," he answered. "His house is open to anyone until mid afternoon and even sometimes on evenings." He offered to send his son with me to show me the house.

A middle-aged woman opened the door. At first, I could only see her large hazel eyes. She was unusually fair-skinned and her hair still kept a bit of blonde in it. She wore a simple black dress, a touch of embroidery on the edges and the chest, and had a light purple beaded scarf tucking her hair back.

"Sorry to disturb you. Is it possible to see the mayor?"

"Ahlan wa sahlan. I am his wife. My name is Haifa. What is your name, my dear?" she asked.

"My name is Majdaleen." I used the original form she would recognise, instead of Madeleine.

She walked me to the diwan. From the door I could see ʿAbdulkarim Younis seated in the centre of the room on a mat with cushions to support his back against the wall. He had a heavy moustache and wore the traditional village headdress of black and white *hatta* and *ʿighal*. The room was carpeted, with mats and cushions on three sides. I removed my shoes and walked toward him.

"As salām ʿalaykum," I greeted.

"Waʿalaykum es salām," he retorted, perhaps surprised that a foreign woman was saying this. He motioned for me to sit down to his left, and we continued with more pleasantries, the usual ones I had learned.

"I hope your trip is bringing you satisfaction, and you like our country."

"Of course, I like the country and the people very much," I said using a cliché to express my true feelings.

Haifa walked in carrying a tray with glasses, a teapot and a plate of dates. She sat on the mat close to me and started pouring.

"What brings us the honour of your visit?"

"I came to ask you if you know anything about events that happened here a long time ago. On the bus the driver told me many people in the village belong to the Younis family. A man born here long ago was called Younis. He was taken as a slave to Siqilya and there started a revolt against the Roman Empire. He led a large army and hundreds of thousands of followers seeking freedom. The revolt lasted for several years. He returned here, sought refuge in Arwad and found home again in that free community on the coast. He would have come back to Afamia at some point, and I'm not sure if he ever returned to live here. Do you know anything about this that would help?"

"When did that happen?"

"More than two thousand years ago." 'Abdulkarim made a "tch" sound in surprise or incredulity as he smiled.

"That's a long time. All I know is that we had an ancestor whose name was Younis after whom we call ourselves. It's a tradition we keep."

"Do you have records that go back?"

"Of course, but they couldn't possibly go back that far. The records I have cover the last hundred and fifty years or so, records of births and deaths and other civic matters. It is said that older papers were consumed in a fire almost two hundred years ago. But even if those records had survived, I doubt they would go back as far as two thousand years."

I sipped the rest of my tea. "I've taken a lot of your time. I should be moving. I would like to visit the sites and find a hotel."

"Stay please," 'Abdukarim said. "It is an important story you tell. It is a source of pride that a man from among us did such great things in the past. Whether he is our ancestor or not does not matter. We are proud of him."

"Yes. That's why I'm trying to find out more to complete his story."

Haifa had begun bringing in trays and placing them on the mat in front of us, first bowls of salad, tabbouleh, various fried vegetables, yogurt, pickles and olives, and hot home-baked bread.

Then she entered carrying the steaming main dish. I recognised it as *maqlubeh*, flavoured rice cooked with layers of eggplant and meat at the bottom, sometimes cauliflower and chicken, then turned over on a large plate or tray, which is why it's called *maqlubeh*, upside down. Mid afternoon is the time for the main meal, I should have known. It was too late to refuse and it would be impolite to leave.

After the meal and cardamom coffee, I told Haifa I wanted to go and see the ruins before sunset. She said it was too far to walk. In no time her son Tareq and his younger brother Ghassan were outside in a banged up old Mercedes. I asked for my travel bag and tried to take it, but Haifa told me it was not time for that.

The Colonnade in Afamia
(Ministry of Tourism, Dimaŝq)

"Tareq will bring you back. You will stay with us tonight. There's no way you'll be allowed to go to a hotel here, and certainly there's no time to take the bus anywhere."

Next morning after breakfast Tareq took me to the bus station. "Consider this place your home. Come to us whenever you're close," said Haifa as we embraced and kissed on the cheek as old friends.

I decided to change my plans. I had wanted to take a bus north to Ḥalab and then to Ras Shamra on the coast to see the ruins of Ugarit, a city whose discovery revealed the polytheistic origin of what we came to call monotheism and, three thousand five hundred years ago, had an alphabet written in cuneiform-like signs with sounds and a vocabulary almost exactly like Arabic. But something told me to delay this trip and instead head back to Dimaŝq and then to ancient Tadmor, what is called Palmyra. After an overnight at a convent in Dimaŝq, I woke up early and took the bus.

In about an hour, we had left behind the buildings, trees, groves and vegetation of Dimaŝq and entered the Syrian Desert, the Badia. It's not a desert in the sense of being an immense pit of sand, but is instead an expanse of dry solid barrenness, what someone more religiously-minded might call desolation. It did not elicit in me any inclination to evade or condemn it. I felt clarity, a freeing openness, rather than fear of its emptiness. Its blankness asked for a response, tempting the self to search for some relief. I wanted instead to embrace its nothingness as a nomadic essence, driven by a longing now more than before for a simplicity that preceded systems and certainties.

The Syrian Badia, Valley of Tombs, Tadmor
(www.vascoplanet.com)

The bus stopped close to the Temple of Baʿal Šāmīn. I approached it from the portico, which had six large columns, topped by acanthus decoration on their capitals. It was a unique integration of classical and regional art. The four front columns had platforms that would have held statues presumably discarded when the temple was converted to a church. Inside the cella, there seemed to be no clear evidence of a church. The slender columns inside were rendered in Corinthian style with the intricate ceiling and shrine designs predominantly in keeping with local tradition. The bracket of one column still featured a dedicatory inscription to a benefactor whose bust must have later been removed.

Being inside the temple brought to mind contradictory images of this enduring god of the heavens and rains, who has been demonised, though still venerated by some or a few, as in isolated remnants of worship in Syria and Lebanon and various

Temple of Baʿal Šāmīn, Tadmor*
(General Directorate of Antiquities, Dimašq)

*Publisher's note: Some of the structures described here were destroyed in 2015.

forms of pagan revival today in the West. It also reminded me of Brecht, who had an image of Baʿal on his bedroom wall, and whose first play about barren modernity and anti-social rebellion against bourgeois morality is entitled *Baal*. How far is such sensibility different from mainstream assumptions in such works as Golding's *Lord of the Flies*, a novel that adopts notions about Beel-zebub as a false god and demon, a huge distortion that converts "zebub" to allude to flies and dirt, when instead it means, as in the New Testament's "Zebul," either "prince" or fertile manured soil that begets a rich harvest.

As I walked down the Great Colonnade, I noticed more columns standing than during my last visit, no doubt the result of recent restoration. Most of the area farther ahead was still littered with broken columns and fragments of statues and friezes in disarray, inviting the observer to imagine what life throbbed around them when they were erect. This would have been the compact centre of the city, with the markets and main dwellings stretching out on either side. Toward the end of the colonnade a pathway to the left looked as if it could have been lined with columns and porticoes. To the right stood Diocletian's Camp and the Temple of Al-Lāt. This camp, it is said, was built on the ruins of the palace of Queen Bit Zabbai, the famous Zenobia. Considering the outline of the city walls, it makes sense for her palace to have been located here, next to the temple of the goddess Al-Lāt, Mother Goddess, Queen of the Heavens, goddess of love and war, and defender of cities. Much of Bit Zabbai's history is not well known, and there's no great memorial left of her deeds, nor a tomb for her end, she who proudly rode at the head of armies and defied empires.

I headed south to the funerary towers. I came first to the Tower of Yemliko, which was locked, then walked west for about twenty minutes toward an area at the edge of a hill with several funerary towers of various sizes. The best preserved and tallest structure was the Tower of Elahbel, which had been restored and was now open to visitors. It was built by Yarhai and named after his father Elahbel, the oldest of the four sons of Ma'ani, as the final resting place for them and their descendants. Its four storeys were constructed from massive sandstones, and it stood twelve metres long and six metres wide and about twenty-four metres high, with an inset arched balcony two-thirds of the way up. Four steps on three sides lead up to the entrance, more than three metres high, ornamented above in pediment and moulding, with an overdoor featuring winged figures and an inscription in Palmyrene Aramaic.

Bit Zabbai (Zenobia)
(Wikimedia Commons)

The chamber on the first storey was about five metres by eight and six metres high with fluted pilasters in each corner. Facing the entrance were tiers of loculi where embalmed bodies would have been sealed, and five busts with carved inscriptions. The ceiling had panels painted in white flowers on a sky-blue background. In the centre of the ceiling, four larger square tiles each bore the portrait of a face whose features had been partially erased. To the left, a steep staircase led up to the upper storeys, and above it more busts would have been arranged with three on top and two below. Counting the number of possible sarcophagi on the first storey one could guess the structure to have lodged as many as one to two hundred bodies.

Elahbel funerary tower
(General Directorate of Antiquities, Dimašq)

I was trying to locate the burial niches of women and men whose busts I had seen in museums and on websites. A few busts were moved to Dimašq, but many were surreptitiously removed by travelers and explorers and some eventually ferreted away in museums in Western cities. I was struck how real and full of character the people looked, like Etruscan statuary, somewhat stylised, probably representing people as younger than their age at death. Standing in the absence of their busts I felt their presence still here, wondering why their images had been dragged so far away. Where is the sarcophagus of Abra, daughter of Zabdila, looking so proud, her tiara intimating ears of wheat, a dove nestling in her left hand? Is she inscribed as "daughter" of her mother because her beauties, her boldness died too young to be fulfilled? Why is Tamma (now at the British Museum), richly attired, holding a spindle and distaff? And Ummayat, daughter of Yarhai, must be here somewhere

Ummayat
(The Louvre)

in her father's tower. Her bust (now at the Louvre) is bedecked in unpretentious jewellery, simple earrings, pearl necklace and tiara. What does the ring in her little finger mean? Why is she holding her hand sadly on her cheek?

Perhaps the one called "the Beauty of Palmyra," since her name is unknown, is buried in this or another tower, we don't know. Whoever cut the block out to remove her bust forgot to include the inscription, or didn't record her name, or couldn't read it, or didn't care. Another unknown is dressed in simple attire and has dreamy eyes and big ears. Why is she one who carries a writing tablet? Was she reading or did she write works that have been lost?

I climbed the steep steps to the third storey and put my head out through the window of the balcony, which looked like a walk-out from a distance but wasn't meant to stand on. I moved back and started to climb the stairs going to the roof, in search of fresh air and a better view. To get to the roof from the last step required some athletic manoeuvres. I was in the process of doing that when an arm stretched out. I looked up at the figure and took the hand.

"It's a difficult one, the last step," the man said in almost perfect English once I stepped on the roof and walked to the edge.

"Yes, thank you." As I stood on the roof and surveyed the desert valley, I could see from the edge of my left eye the man starting down the stairs. His features seemed vaguely familiar, a face slightly bearded, nose prominent and dark curly hair almost to the shoulders. "My name is Samer," he said as he was going down. "If you want, I'll wait downstairs and we can walk together." I nodded and gave him my name. Curiously, his name is not dissimilar in meaning from that of the man I wrote about.

I liked it that I was left alone on the roof. We walked back into the valley. It took more than an hour to reach the fortress, back toward the ruins and then up a steep escarpment. I did not have any tiredness from such a hard walk in the heat of the day. Nor did I feel any emptiness in the desert expanse. Its unknown spirits called me to a new search.

SLAVE KING

ABOUT THE AUTHOR

Basem Lutfi Ra'ad, a Professor (PhD, Toronto), has taught at universities in Canada and abroad, mostly in Palestine and Lebanon. He initiated community and academic projects, organized international conferences, and published in major journals, including *PMLA, Modern Fiction Studies* and *American Literature*, on topics such as literature, linguistics, landscape aesthetics, cultural studies, travel writing, and political issues. His book *Hidden Histories: Palestine and the Eastern Mediterranean*, which also appeared in Arabic, provides an alternative reading of the long history of a region commonly called "the Middle East," "the cradle of civilization," and "the Holy Land," that emphasizes continuities among its people and discredits old and new myths using recent scholarship. Its chapters cover ancient history, development of polytheistic and monotheistic religions, invention of religious sites, regional civilizational accomplishments, Ugarit, writing systems, and present reflections on such subjects as identity, appropriation, self-colonization, place names, and retrieval of cultural heritage. The book has been described by critics as "perhaps the first corrective history of Palestine," "a brilliant tour de force of recovery, de-colonization, re-vision and inclusivity." Among his current writings are various literary projects and studies of regional school curricula and tourist information to assess their contents in relation to contemporary scholarship and a coherent historical/ cultural narrative.

www.ingramcontent.com/pod-product-compliance
Lightning Source LLC
Chambersburg PA
CBHW050128030726
47505CB00007B/2079